P9-CZV-745

"Keri? Are you sitting down? It's about Justin Kramer."

It had been some years since detective Keri Mahoney had heard her first love's name, but it had cropped up only too often in recent weeks. Her sister Raven's phone call got her full attention. "What about him?"

"I think the Kansas City police are getting close to an arrest. Justin and his lawyer spent the better part of the afternoon in an interrogation room with the detectives working his wife's homicide."

"I just can't believe it," Keri breathed, almost to herself.

"I absolutely *don't* believe it," Raven said emphatically. "Justin Kramer is no killer."

"Not when he was fourteen, you mean." But considering he never bothered to keep in touch after his family's move, how could Keri really know if he was capable of murder at the ripe old age of twenty-nine?

* * *

The Mahoney Sisters: Fighting for justice and love.

REASONABLE DOUBT, August 2005
SUSPICION OF GUILT, September 2005
BETRAYAL OF TRUST, October 2005

TRACEY V. BATEMAN

lives in Missouri with her husband and their four children. She writes full-time and is active in various roles in her home church. She has won several awards for her writing and credits God's grace and a limited number of entries for each win. To relax, she enjoys long talks with her husband, reading and music and hanging out with her kids, who can finally enjoy movies she likes. Tracey loves to encourage everyone to dream big. She believes she is living proof that, with God, nothing is impossible.

Reasonable Doubt

Tracey V. Bateman

Steeple Hill®

Published by Steeple Hill Books™

If you purchased this book without a cover you should be aware that this book is stolen property. It was reported as "unsold and destroyed" to the publisher, and neither the author nor the publisher has received any payment for this "stripped book."

STEEPLE HILL BOOKS

Steeple
Hill®

ISBN 0-373-44220-3

REASONABLE DOUBT

Copyright © 2005 by Tracey V. Bateman

All rights reserved. Except for use in any review, the reproduction or utilization of this work in whole or in part in any form by any electronic, mechanical or other means, now known or hereafter invented, including xerography, photocopying and recording, or in any information storage or retrieval system, is forbidden without the written permission of the editorial office, Steeple Hill Books, 233 Broadway, New York, NY 10279 U.S.A.

All characters in this book have no existence outside the imagination of the author and have no relation whatsoever to anyone bearing the same name or names. They are not even distantly inspired by any individual known or unknown to the author, and all incidents are pure invention.

This edition published by arrangement with Steeple Hill Books.

® and TM are trademarks of Steeple Hill Books, used under license. Trademarks indicated with ® are registered in the United States Patent and Trademark Office, the Canadian Trade Marks Office and in other countries.

www.SteepleHill.com

Printed in U.S.A.

"For I know the plans I have for you,"
says the Lord. "They are plans for good and
not for disaster, to give you a future and a hope."
—*Jeremiah* 29:11

Dedicated to my niece Amanda Guidry.
Thanks for your editorial input and practical,
commonsense ideas as I put the proposal together
for this book. You are so talented. I look forward
to watching as God unfolds your future.

Chapter One

Justin Kramer knew two things for certain.

One, he hadn't murdered his wife.

Two, the detectives weren't buying it.

The four-month-old memory of Amelia's body lying facedown on the blue living-room carpet was etched as a horrifying image in his mind. An image Justin knew he wouldn't shake for the rest of his life—which, if the cops had their way, would be spent up the river, without possibility of parole.

The detectives stood over him like a couple of lions working together to bring down a zebra. Justin's glare swept them both. "What do you think my wife's killer is doing while you two are playing good cop/bad cop for the third time?"

Detective Raney slapped his hands flat on the table and rested his considerable weight on tree trunk-like arms. He leaned forward and stared Justin square in the eye.

Disgusted, Justin clamped his lips together and shifted backward. The guy's breath stank of cigarettes and coffee—one or the other was enough to gag a horse. Together they were nothing less than cruel and unusual punishment.

The detective pressed forward to close the distance caused by Justin's not-so-subtle retreat. "Just shut your smart mouth and answer the questions."

Without even trying to hide his amusement, Justin twisted his lips. "I can't shut my mouth and answer the questions at the same time." He knew he sounded like a juvenile delinquent, but he was getting pretty sick of being accused of murder when he'd done nothing worse than allow Amelia to run all over him for years.

Detective Appling clapped his partner on the shoulder, effectively getting him out of Justin's immediate air space.

Appling's face molded into an amiable expression—one obviously carefully practiced and intended to instill confidence in the would-be criminal. "Come on, Justin. Don't you think it's time to tell the truth?"

The good-cop routine was getting old. Justin leveled his gaze at Appling. "Didn't you two switch roles? Seems like last time you hauled me in for questioning, you were the heavy."

Detective Appling's eyes glittered hard. His lips tensed and turned down at the corners. He perched on the edge of the table, no longer playing a pal. "Let's talk about where you were the night your wife was killed. Say…around eleven-thirty."

"He's told you where he was. Repeatedly." Bob Landau, a friend and the only attorney Justin knew, sat in a chair at the other end of the table, looking a lot more comfortable than he had any right to while Justin's freedom dangled from a worn-out thread.

Justin's call had interrupted a workout, so the lawyer had gunned it over to the police station without bothering to change out of a pair of sweats, running shoes and a sweatshirt. Nor had he bothered to remove his Chicago White Sox baseball cap. In Kansas City Royals territory that act alone was practically criminal.

Detective Raney sneered at Bob. He snagged a metal chair leg with his booted toes and pulled it out. With a grunt he plopped into the seat. "I'm tired of getting the same answer."

Too bad for him. Justin only had one answer to give—the truth. "For the third time, I was at the Victory Mission Men's Shelter. All night. I didn't leave until a little after six the next morning."

He'd never forget sitting up with Ike Rawlings all night while the alcoholic shook and vomited out his addiction. Only Jesus had gotten them through those horrific hours. In the morning, Ike had surrendered to Christ. Chills still crawled up Justin's spine at the awe of a life changed. God's love and glory manifested in one life-changing moment.

Raney jerked his head at Justin and picked up a manila file folder from the table. He waved it under Justin's nose like a plate of filet mignon. "Know what I have here?"

"Not a clue. But I have a feeling you're going to tell me."

In one fluid movement, the officer slapped the file open on the table with the flat of his hand, keeping the bottom of the page covered. "Signed testimony from two men who say you left during the night and came back later."

Triumph gleamed in the detective's eyes. Closing the file, he leaned back, lacing pudgy fingers over his ample gut.

Unwilling to give Raney the satisfaction of knowing how badly the news had rattled him, Justin forced himself to keep a bland expression. "You're bluffing."

The officer glared over the rim of an enormous coffee mug. He set the cup back down, gathered a long, slow breath and started again. "The cards are stacked against you, Kramer." He held up his thumb then one finger and another as he counted off the marks against Justin. "A murdered woman, no sign of forced entry and there are witnesses who demolish your alibi. And, I have to tell you, those separate bedrooms don't exactly speak of marital bliss."

Bob shifted forward. "Why don't you guys give him a break? You haven't even charged him with a crime."

"Yet."

The smirk on the cop's face touched a raw nerve, but Justin knew he had to stay calm—not give in to the goading.

Detective Appling scrubbed at his bristled face and half sighed, half growled, obviously disappointed not to have rattled him. "You went to the shelter and waited until everyone fell asleep. Then you snuck out, strangled your wife and got back before anyone knew you'd gone. Not bad for a rookie killer."

"What makes you think I'm a rookie?" Justin had meant to be flippant—a knee-jerk response to the ridiculous assumptions. Big mistake.

The officer leaned in, his brow arched. "Is that a confession?"

"Hey! Objection!" Bob's hand smacked down hard on the cheap, plastic-veneer tabletop.

Shifting his gaze to Bob, Appling cut a look that was nothing less than derisive. "Give *me* a break. This isn't a courtroom."

Bob shot from his chair. "Do you realize that Mr. Kramer's cooperation is voluntary?"

"We hear you, Mr. Landau. But we have a good reason for questioning him about his so-called alibi. And like you said, he agreed to the questions, so he might as well answer the right ones, or there's really no point, is there?"

"Just watch how you phrase your sentences. I'd hate to slap you with a lawsuit."

"Sure you would." The officer turned his attention back to Justin. "See, one problem with your version of the story is that your drunk can't be found for questioning."

"You know where he is. I already told you."

"Refresh my memory."

Justin knew they were testing him. Would he give the same story he'd told them twice already? Or would the details change? Carefully, he conjured the memory of Ike's battle that night.

"I wanted him to stay for a few weeks to rehabilitate, take some Bible classes, but he insisted. Said he needed to get a job as soon as possible and take care of his family. So I put him on a bus to Chicago."

"So you said, but we can't find any Ike Rawlings in Chicago."

Justin shrugged. "It's my fault you're not much of a detective?"

The detective's lips curled into a sneer. "Watch yourself, Kramer. At the very least, the Chicago PD should be able to find him. But so far, no phone listing, no electric bills issued to Ike Rawlings. As a matter of fact, we've checked every Rawlings in the Chicago area, and nada."

"He could have been using a phony name, I guess. Lots of the men who come to the mission do that." It was a thin suggestion, Justin knew, and the detective's short laugh proved it.

"Okay, sure…phony name, and the guy conveniently left town so that there's no tracing him. Not much of an alibi to refute our witnesses."

"You keep talking about witnesses, but I didn't see any signatures."

"And you're not going to."

Bob grabbed his briefcase from the floor next to his vacated chair. "I think you've taken enough of Mr. Kramer's time today, so unless you plan to arrest him, we're going to walk out of here now."

The detectives exchanged looks that clearly revealed their reluctance to let him go. Justin's stomach churned.

A scowl twisted Detective Raney's fat face. "Get out of here," he snarled, his breath assaulting Justin's air space once more.

Justin balled his fists to keep his hands from trembling. "I'm free to go?"

"For now."

Feeling his bravado crumbling, Justin rose on shaky legs and followed Bob, praying to God he wouldn't pass out before he made it through the door.

They walked shoulder to shoulder down the long hallway. A blast of cold air shot into the building as Bob opened the heavy glass doors. In the parking lot, Justin expelled a pent-up breath. He shook his head. "I don't get why anyone would say I left the center that night, when I didn't. Do you think it's a case of mistaken identity?"

"No," Bob replied in a flat, hard tone. "I think someone is setting you up. There's no telling what evidence has been planted the police haven't run across yet. But eventually, they're going to find a convenient piece of proof that you killed Amelia."

"But I didn't."

"You and I know that. And whoever killed her knows it, but that won't convince a jury. Eyewitnesses and circumstantial evidence convince juries. The cops have those things. We have nothing."

Deputy Keri Mahoney opened her mouth wide to take a bite of her on-the-go burger when her cell phone rang to the tune of "Deep in the Heart of Texas." She jumped, and ketchup escaped the bun, globbing onto her uniform before she could stop it. "Great." Why had she ever allowed Dad's southern-belle fiancée to program that stupid song into the phone? It nearly sent her through the roof every time it rang.

Negotiating the hamburger to prevent another glob of ketchup from plopping onto her clothes, she tried to snatch her cell at the same time. Impossible. With a growl, she pulled into the nearest parking lot and located the phone.

"Yes?"

"Kere?"

Swiping at the ketchup stain on her tan slacks, Keri scowled.

"Who else?" she barked.

"Sheesh. Did you get up on the wrong side of the bed or what?" Her sister Raven's voice only irritated her more, but she fought to keep her temper in check.

"What's up, Rave?"

"Are you sitting down?"

"Yeah, I'm in the Jeep."

"It's about Justin Kramer."

She stopped swiping and gave Raven her full attention. "What about him?"

"I think the KC police are getting close to an arrest."

Swallowing past the sudden thickness in her throat, Keri managed to croak, "How do you know?"

"Eugene. Who else?" Raven's contact at the Kansas City PD. A dispatcher with a crush on the annoyingly gorgeous TV reporter.

"Is it still off the record?"

"Yeah, for now. But he said Justin and his lawyer spent the better part of the afternoon in an interrogation room with the detectives working his wife's homicide."

"I just can't believe it," she breathed, almost to herself.

No longer in the mood for lunch, Keri wrapped her barely eaten sandwich and stuffed it back in the bag.

"I absolutely *don't* believe it," Raven said emphatically. "Justin Kramer is no killer."

"Not when he was fourteen, you mean." But considering he'd never bothered to come back as he'd said he would, how could she really know if he was capable of murder at the ripe old age of twenty-nine?

* * *

"She can't make you go. It's not fair."

Fourteen-year-old Keri Mahoney sat on the bank overlooking Bennett Lake and swiped at the tears on her freckled cheeks. She stared glumly at the shallow, gray water gurgling over opaque brown stones in the summer breeze. The brilliant sun reflected off the creek—a mocking contrast to the dismal reality stretching before her.

Justin Kramer sat beside her, equally sullen, snapping twigs and tossing them into the water. One by one the pieces disappeared, carried away by the current. Keri knew exactly how they felt. Helpless, hopeless… drowning.

Justin sighed. "Aunt Toni says we might come back for a visit sometime." But his voice didn't offer much hope, as if he couldn't quite convince himself they'd ever see each other again.

"Who am I going to talk to when you're gone?" She hugged her knees to her chest and buried her face in the rough denim of her jeans. "You're the only friend I have."

"You still have Jesus." The statement might have sounded stupid coming from anyone else, but Justin's words rang with sincerity. Keri had the familiar, unsettling sense that Justin knew God as no one else did— better than she did, anyway.

Feeling the warmth of his palm on her back, she looked up, drinking in his tender expression, memorizing the smooth contours of his handsome face. Black hair, freshly cut, swept across his forehead and around his ears. His nose was just wide enough to even out his face, and his square jaw made him the most handsome boy in class. Not one eighth-grade girl could dispute that fact.

Keri couldn't help the pride that accompanied her relationship with Justin. She barely gave a thought to her own looks when Justin looked at her. He never mentioned her freckles, skinny legs or coarse, orange hair. Every girl wanted to be pretty, but Justin didn't care if she wasn't, so Keri didn't, either. Not much.

Beautiful blue eyes pierced her very soul. Words had never been necessary between them. Even now, though he didn't speak, Keri knew he was thinking about his parents. How could he not, when the only life he'd ever known had been snuffed out along with their lives only a week ago?

Why did God have to take both of his parents away? Why couldn't at least one of them have survived the car accident?

"Justin!" Hidden by the trees surrounding the creek, they heard Justin's aunt calling from the cabin. "Where are you? It's time to go."

Justin's hand tightened around hers, and Keri rested her head on his shoulder. He slipped his arm around her, drawing her close. It was the first time he'd done that, and Keri felt her heart pound at the grown-up gesture.

Rather than feeling awkward, it felt right, as though she belonged in his embrace. She'd always thought they'd marry some day. Only now…now he was going away.

"Promise you won't forget Jesus," he said, his voice barely more than a whisper.

Keri's heart sank. For once, why couldn't he talk about something personal? Confess undying love. *Kiss her.* She loved Jesus, too, but there was a time and a place.

"Justin Michael Kramer, get up here this instant or you're going to be in big trouble, young man!"

Reluctance clouded his eyes and he pulled away. "I guess I better go before she explodes a vein."

A sense of panic swelled inside Keri. She grabbed at his black T-shirt. "Kiss me goodbye, Justin." His startled gaze met hers just before she closed her eyes and lifted her chin.

Feather-soft lips brushed across hers. Never had Keri experienced the feelings springing to life in her heart in that moment. Justin, her friend, her hero and now the first boy ever to kiss her. It seemed right.

Only his aunt interrupted the beautiful moment. "Justin!"

He pulled away and jumped to his feet. A long silent stare followed, then he sprinted toward the edge of the woods.

"I love you," Keri called after him. "I won't forget you, I promise."

He turned. "I'll be back," he promised before disappearing into the trees.

"I'll wait," she whispered. "I'll never forget you."

The squeal of tires accosted Keri's attention and she jerked around. A blur of red shot past the parking lot, weaving down the road. Horns blared as the pickup narrowly missed a black sedan and a blue hatchback.

"Gotta go, Rave."

"What do you mean you have to—"

Making a grab for the strobe light, Keri punched off the phone and switched on her siren. Junior Connor— already drunk at 7:00 p.m.—was headed for the bar, which meant he'd brought along his own booze. Mentally, she racked up the charges, from DUI to open container, to manslaughter if she didn't get to him before he got to that group of teens hanging out on the corner.

Anger boiled her blood as she slammed the SUV into gear and burned out after the pickup. She wasn't about to sit by and let that lush take out someone's kid. Not on her watch.

Red digital numbers glared; it was just past midnight. Punching his pillow, Justin let out a half growl as he replayed today's interrogation over and over in his head. He was sick of being called in for questioning by those goons, sick of not knowing who had killed Amelia, and even more sick of being the only suspect the police seemed to have.

Helplessness sliced at his gut like a dagger. So far, he'd sat back and done pretty much nothing while the detectives worked to find anything to pin Amelia's murder on his shoulders. He was a sitting duck, just waiting to be arrested for a murder he didn't commit.

Releasing a heavy sigh, he flopped over. Lacing his fingers behind his head, he stared toward the ceiling. He needed a vacation. A long, peaceful vacation somewhere away from the media attention, away from the stress of the city and wondering each morning if this might be the day when his worst nightmare became a reality. He closed his eyes, and his mind conjured the image of the only vacation spot he'd ever known.

Until his parents' deaths, he'd spent time every summer at the Mahoney cabin on Lake Bennett. He could almost smell the crisp clean lake, could almost see the sun reflecting off wind-rippled water. A flash of freckles on cheeks just below enormous green eyes joined the nostalgic images. His girl. His lips curved upward as he finally succumbed to his fatigue and drifted to sleep.

Justin awoke slowly, battling the fading images of a sweet, sweet dream, one he didn't want to forget. He fought to remember a face surrounded by riotous red curls, and pea-green eyes invaded his consciousness.

"Keri," he whispered into the still-darkened room. He sat up.

Determination sent a jolt through his stomach. He was going to do it! Take the boys on a vacation like the ones he'd enjoyed growing up. The Mahoney cabin at Lake Bennett. The twins would love the lake. Too bad it wasn't summertime. Trout fishing and cutoff shorts were out of the question this time of year, but even in winter, a couple of nine-year-old boys would find plenty to pique their interest.

He couldn't bear the thought of the boys spending Thanksgiving in the house where their mother had been murdered. Josh's outbursts and nightmares were getting worse. The kid definitely needed a little time away. By this time next year, he hoped, they would be able to put the house on the market and begin the process of putting all of this behind them. He prayed so.

Justin raked his fingers through hair that could have used a pair of scissors three weeks ago. The police had never told him he was under any kind of restriction to stay in Kansas City. He supposed it was implied, possibly understood. But certainly not mandated.

At a sudden *ping, ping* against the window, he pushed back the covers, swung his legs over the side of the bed and walked across the freezing wooden floor.

His gut clenched as he recognized the falling ice. If he waited much longer, the curvy roads between here and the cabin might not be drivable. On a good day, it was a two-hour drive. If this weather didn't let up, he was looking at three, four, maybe five hours.

The red digital numbers on the bedside clock glowed 4:30 a.m. Too early to call Mr. Mahoney and ask about using the cabin. He'd try to find a number to call once he was on the road. If he couldn't rent the Mahoney cabin, there were several others on the lake, a couple of them rentals, as he recalled. Grabbing a suitcase from the closet, he slung it on the bed and started packing.

Fifteen years. That's how long he'd been away. He couldn't help but remember that last day sitting with Keri on the bank overlooking the lake. He smiled at the memory of her sweet kiss. A first for them both.

Was she still in Briarwood? He didn't count on seeing her, not in this weather and considering the cabin was at least an hour's drive away from the small town where he'd spent the first fourteen years of his life. Still, the memories were sweet, and he couldn't help but wonder how her life had panned out. Better than his, he hoped.

The twins mumbled their displeasure when he woke them a few moments later.

"Where're we going, Dad?" Billy asked with a yawn.

"You'll find out." He settled the boys at the kitchen

table. Made them toast, then snatched a leftover ham from the fridge. Just as he started to slice through the meat to make sandwiches for the road, a thud caught his attention, he turned and felt the pain in his finger as the blade nicked the tender flesh of his thumb.

He winced. "What happened?"

"Billy fell out of his chair."

"You all right, Billy?"

The child sat up on the floor, sleepy-eyed but nodding. "I'm okay."

"You're bleeding, Dad." Josh's voice rang with tension.

Justin glanced at his throbbing finger. Blood dripped onto the floor. He turned quickly to the sink and ran his finger under the water, grateful it wasn't a deep cut. He grabbed a bandage and covered the wound.

When he turned back around, Josh had wiped up the blood from the floor. However, the boy's face had also lost all color and he sat holding the rag in his hand.

"Here, give me that, son."

Josh relinquished the cloth and turned away.

With a sigh, Justin ruffled his head. "You two get some movies and toys. Only what will fit in your schoolbags."

He watched them, Billy scrambling with his usual fervor, Josh slinking away as though he couldn't care less.

A wave of helplessness washed over Justin. Nothing seemed to help Josh cope with the events of the past months. Counseling hadn't helped. Not so far, anyway. Church wasn't restoring the child's soul. Yet he believed God was faithful. He had built a life and ministry on that belief. Once he'd returned to God, he would have built his marriage on the same belief if Amelia had been open. But religion was never her thing, as she reminded him every time he tried to talk to her about God.

If only she'd listened. Maybe she'd still be alive.

Chapter Two

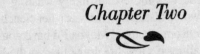

"Let's get one thing straight, Junior. No one made you crawl behind that wheel and drive drunk." The barred door clanged shut with the same finality that rang in Deputy Keri Mahoney's voice. "You're in jail because you deserve it, so stop whining."

"You just ain't got no compassion in your soul." Hours after his arrest for drunk driving, Junior Connor's words were still slurred, doing little to strengthen his case with Keri. "But I don't guess I should expect no more from a power-hungry female, doin' a man's job."

Keri ignored the familiar comment. She was accustomed to the fact that most of the men in Briarwood, Missouri, hadn't progressed past 1950 in terms of male/female relationships. But that wasn't Junior's only problem. He was a drunk. Keri had no tolerance for drunks, thugs or idiots who ran red lights through school zones. Junior embodied all three.

"Drinking and driving kills people. You remember my mama, don't you?"

"Sure, I remember her. Fine woman." He snorted. "Too bad you ain't got none of her qualities."

Keri stomped back across the lemony-clean concrete floor and glared at him through the bars. He'd already made it to his bunk and his eyelids were half shut, so she knew she was more than likely wasting her breath, but the words hissed from between her clenched teeth like steam from a kettle. "Maybe I'd have gotten some of her qualities if a low-life drunk like you hadn't killed her before she had the chance to teach me."

He opened one eye and shot up straight from his cot. "You know good and well I ain't never killed no one. Ain't even all that drunk, if you wanna know the truth of it." He pointed his gnarly finger. "You didn't have no call to go arresting me in the first place. I got half a mind to sue the department."

Disgusted, Keri didn't trust herself to answer. If Junior didn't shut up pretty soon, she might have to accidentally toss the key to his cell out the window.

"You hear me, girl? I'll sue you and this whole department. I'll own the town before it's all over."

"Go ahead and sue, if you can get your lawyer to return your phone calls." She spun around and headed back to the twenty-five-year-old metal desk, where a stack of paperwork and an extra-large pumpkin cappuccino from the local Quick Shop awaited her. If only Junior would go to sleep and give her some peace and quiet, she'd have it all done before her shift ended at 7:00 a.m. Then she had two weeks of vacation coming.

Dad had suggested—no, downright *insisted*—she

take her two weeks this year, even if he had to sneak out and flatten all four of her tires once they got to the cabin to make sure she stuck to the bargain. He didn't have to worry about that. For now, she needed solace. Quiet. Time for reflection.

Given her history of taking working vacations, Keri had to admit her dad was right to be skeptical. But this year things were going to be different. Her resolve was strong. Under no circumstance was she going to stay home where the chief could drag her out of the house with some flimsy excuse again, as he had every year since she'd joined the force.

With a weary sigh she plopped into her chair and rolled up to the desk. She scowled at the mountain-high stack of papers. As the only full-time deputy in Briarwood for the past ten years, she held a dead-end job in a dead-end town, and as far as Keri could see, looming before her was a dead-end future unless she could somehow convince the all-male city council that she would be a good replacement for Chief Manning when he retired at the end of the year.

She balled her fist, ready to pound the desk at the unfairness of generations of chauvinism, but then she thought better of it as Junior's loud snoring sawed through the air. No sense taking a chance on waking him up—not if she intended to get through months of neglected paperwork.

Just why the town couldn't dig up the money for a new jail with an up-to-date computer system when they had recently spent ten thousand dollars on park beautification, she couldn't fathom. Instead the good folks of Briarwood were stuck with an Andy Griffith jail, and she and Chief Manning were the Andy and Barney jokes of the town.

Keri sipped a frothy taste of her pumpkin cappuccino. She sighed as the sweet spices licked her taste buds and tempted her memory with pictures of holiday mealtimes at the Mahoney house. She could picture them all sitting around the cherrywood dining table: her two sisters, Dad and Mom.

Holidays never were quite the same after Mom died. Nothing was the same. Keri was finishing up high school, but her older sisters Raven and Denni were already in college by then. She was alone. If only Justin hadn't moved away, he'd have been there for her during that time, and who knew where her life might have ended up?

Impatiently, Keri dropped the drink cup into the wastebasket, as if to toss away the memories, but they persisted. And at the thought of her childhood sweetheart, the memory of Raven's wretched phone call floated through her mind.

Keri's gut tightened. Was Justin a murderer?

The heater fan roared to life, bringing her back to the present and to Junior's whining.

"That thing woke me up. If I don't get enough sleep I'll get a headache."

"Tough. This isn't a hotel."

"I could sue you for violation of my civil rights. And don't think I ain't got a good lawyer."

"Yeah, a real good lawyer who couldn't get you out of jail and won't return your calls," Keri muttered.

He didn't respond right away, and Keri found herself alone with her memories once again. The thought of her Justin harming anyone, let alone committing murder was almost impossible for Keri to fathom, despite her years as a police officer.

"I need an aspirin. My head's killing me."

"Be quiet, Junior," she said without looking up. "I'm busy."

There had to be a reasonable explanation. Justin wouldn't kill anyone. Not her Justin. Someone was making a terrible mistake.

At least that's what Keri hoped. A desperate hope. She needed to believe him innocent. If the same gentle Justin who had saved her from bullies and brought her flowers and shared her one and only kiss was a wife murderer, she might as well let Junior out of his cell, hand him a bottle of booze and throw him the keys to his truck. Better yet, maybe she should just join him on his next binge. Belly up to the bar, boys. Here's to the end of all my dreams....

Tears pushed at her eyes, but she blinked them away, and forced herself to focus on her paperwork. She made it through the end of the stack before Chief Manning walked through the door at 7:00 a.m.

"Morning, Deputy."

"Morning."

"I'm sure glad you're here, Sam," Junior called from his cell. "That girl ain't got no heart. I been askin' for an aspirin for the last hour, and she's been ignorin' me. Now I got me a headache the size of the Grand Canyon. I got half a mind to sue you both for prisoner abuse."

Chief Manning took the medicine kit down from the wall and chuckled. "Junior, if you sued us for all the things you threaten, you'd be a millionaire." He grabbed a paper cup, filled it with water from the bathroom faucet, and crossed the room. "Here. Take this and be quiet for a while before you give *me* a headache."

Junior took the aspirin and water through the bars and grumbled all the way back to his bunk.

Keri bit back a snide remark. The guy had been arrested for disorderly conduct and public drunkenness so many times he was a regular fixture at the jail. This time it was different, though. He'd nearly hit those kids. As it was, he'd wrapped his truck around a telephone pole.

The stunned group of teens milling about the accident scene, with shock-white expressions on their faces, had effectively squelched her last remnant of mercy for the likes of Junior Connor.

Why didn't drunk drivers ever kill themselves instead of innocent people?

She slid the last completed file into place, resisting the urge to slap her hands together to dust them off. Two weeks of solitude awaited her, and she had every intention of using the time to reflect, pray and discover exactly what God was trying to show her by sending discontent into her life. She'd tried to escape its iron jaws, but it gripped her unerringly and Keri was powerless to stop the pain. The melancholy persisted no matter how hard she tried, how long she prayed or how many miles she jogged.

"Keri?"

"What?" Keri blinked back to reality at the chief's gruff call.

"I asked if anything happened tonight."

With a sniff, she sent a dismissive wave toward the cell. "No. Just Junior's whining. Most of the paperwork is finished."

"You still plan on spending your vacation at the cabin?"

"I sure am," Keri said, defenses on high alert. "This is our first time at the cabin in years. No phones, no faxes and no radio except in the Jeep, so don't even think about trying to weasel me out of my vacation this year. I need it, Chief. Dad's already up there. Even Denni and Raven are coming up to the cabin for Thanksgiving Day."

He heaved a heavy sigh and lowered himself to the chair with a grunt. "I know you need it, honey. I just have trouble getting along without you."

Keri grabbed her coat from the rack behind the desk. "Better tell that to the town council, because if I don't get your job when you retire, I'm quitting for good. Besides, Abe will do fine filling in for me." The part-time deputy was just itching to spend a couple of weeks in her place.

"Well, you take care out there in those woods."

"Thanks. I will."

"You going over to the café before you head up there?"

"Yeah." Though her stomach rumbled, Keri found it difficult to muster much enthusiasm for the greasy breakfast her future stepmother was undoubtedly preparing at the moment. Just like every other morning.

Maybe she wouldn't go after all. Maybe she'd just grab a donut at the Quick Shop on her way out of town. She wanted change, didn't she? She'd start with breakfast. Then, who knew what else? Maybe she'd dye her hair black and get some fake nails. Nah.

Still, a change of pace sounded great. A change of pace that included, for instance, a promotion and a nice fat raise in pay. Then maybe next year she could afford a trip to Maui for her two-week vacation. She smiled at the thought.

"What are you smiling about? I know it can't be the thought of your stepmother's eggs."

The chief's words brought Keri back from her daydream. "Ruth's not my stepmother yet. And if Dad doesn't stop stalling, she's likely to get fed up with waiting and head back to Texas."

He actually snorted. "I doubt that."

"You never know. Some women don't wait around forever." *Like I have.*

Keri pushed back the melancholy threatening to settle over her once again. She patted the chief's meaty shoulder and headed for the door. "You have everything you need. Abe's capable of holding down the fort. Just remind him to check the radio every now and then to make sure it's switched on." The three-hundred-pound part-timer was notorious for knocking against the switch and shutting off the radio.

The chief chuckled. "Will do."

Keri stepped into the frigid mid-November morning. The brisk air smelled clean, fresh. She gathered in as much as her lungs would hold, then released the breath with a smile, suddenly wide-awake. She glanced at the sky. Pregnant clouds promised the first snowfall of the year, a little earlier than normal, but not a record by any means. Forecasters called for up to eight inches before evening. From the looks of it, old Tom, the weather guy, might have hit the bull's-eye this time.

Wrapping her arms about herself to stop the shivering, she headed toward the café before remembering her decision to eat a donut. She heaved a sigh. She was definitely in a rut.

Barely noticing the familiar insurance building, the thrift store, the General Dollar, she continued toward Ruth's Café.

Her mind whirled, her heart a tumult of emotions as her thoughts returned to Justin. If she were to be perfectly honest with herself, she wasn't sure what ticked her off more, the possibility of him murdering his wife, or the fact that he'd married someone else in the first place.

His see-into-her-soul eyes invaded her mind, and Keri could almost feel the featherlight touch of his lips on hers—the sweetest of memories.

Even after fifteen years, she felt as though she were betraying him for even considering the possibility that he might be guilty. Love, as strong as ever, combined with aching heartbreak at the thought that Justin was somewhere in trouble, and she couldn't help him. Worse still was the nagging worry that he might have actually committed the murder.

As much as her heart rejected the thought, the realist in her had to admit that anyone was capable of changing for the worse. The drunk driver who'd killed her mother was proof of that. If a man could fall off the wagon after years of sobriety and slam his car into an innocent mother of three, a clean-cut teenager could grow up to be a killer.

She'd been following Justin's case through the papers and regular reports from Raven. Raven was sure he'd be declared innocent any moment, but Keri had to wonder. After all these months, an innocent man surely would have been cleared by now.

"Hey, Keri, honey, where you going?"

Keri stopped short and turned at the soft Texas drawl. Her dad's fiancée, Ruth, stood in the café door looking at Keri as though she'd lost her mind. Heat rose to Keri's cheeks. "Sorry," she said, retracing her steps. "I was just spacing, I guess."

"Just wait until you're my age, you'll be lucky to find your shoes. Get yourself in here and eat your breakfast."

Meekly, Keri followed, but her mind drifted back to Justin. Had he been charged with the crime?

Please, God. Take care of him and see him through this trouble he's somehow gotten himself into.

Despite the treacherous driving conditions, Justin couldn't help the excitement he felt as each mile brought him closer to the cabin. He hadn't seen the Mahoney cabin since his parents' death fifteen years earlier. Despite Aunt Toni's promise that she'd take him back there for vacations, she'd promptly forbidden any contact with his past. Said it made him mopey thinking about his old home and that made for bad karma. By the time she was out of her karma phase, Justin had moved on with a new circle of friends.

It hadn't taken Justin long to figure out that Aunt Toni never took vacations. She worked sixteen hours a day every day except for weekends when she shacked up with her most recent boyfriend and left Justin with cash for pizza and movie rentals. By the time he'd graduated high school and moved on to college, Justin hadn't even wanted to go back to Briarwood.

That wasn't true exactly.

He didn't have the guts to face Keri Mahoney after all the promises they'd made each other. He pictured her exactly the way he'd left her. Fresh, wholesome, eyes wide with wonder and hope. Pure.

His back wheels slid and Justin brought his attention back to the highway, which was quickly becoming snow- and ice-covered.

The curvy, hilly highway became treacherous with nearly zero visibility by the time he found the country road leading to the cabin. He breathed a sigh of relief when the landscape began to look vaguely familiar. Just a few miles into the woods, and they'd be safely tucked away from it all.

Chapter Three

Plump flakes of fairy-tale snow gave way to a wintry mix, and ice pellets bounced off the hood of the Jeep. Keri held her breath and prayed. With extra caution, she maneuvered the vehicle onto Highway 13, wishing she hadn't taken the time to go home and change out of her uniform.

Snow-frosted trees lined the winding road with breathtaking beauty. She loved the picturesque view from this road during any season, but the winter scene was her favorite. How could something so beautiful be so potentially fatal?

She tried to keep her thoughts focused on the frozen pavement, but her mind drifted toward Justin as it often did. Rarely did a day go by without memories of her childhood friend invading her consciousness and even her dreams.

Now, she imagined him once again sitting beside her, next to the lake, tossing sticks into the water. The promises, the kiss, the declarations of unending love.

Keri fought her way back from the bittersweet memory that was worlds away from the reality of a treacherous road. With the wipers barely making a difference, she was forced to roll down the window and stick her head out to see the turnoff. Ice pelted her face and stung her eyes. She eased the Jeep onto the gravelly path. Krahoney Road. Despite her precarious situation, a smile tipped her lips. She and Justin had dubbed it that—a combination of their two last names. Keri sobered and focused her attention back to driving a straight course as her back wheels slid to the right. Gasping a prayer, she eased into the slide just in time to avoid the three-foot ditch.

When she was only a couple of miles from the cabin, she noticed faint red lights flashing ahead. She squinted, trying to make out the source of the glow. Recognizing the flashings as hazard lights, she prepared to stop.

Anxiety burst through her veins, sending a warning of caution to her brain. Who in their right mind would be out in this weather and on Krahoney Road in the first place? As far as she knew, no one had been out here since this summer when Dad had commissioned all the remodeling for the cabin.

She eased the Jeep to a stop and started to open the door. Then, just to be safe, she grabbed her gun from the glove box and stuffed it in her belt, behind her back. Cop or not, a woman alone on a deserted road was still at a disadvantage to a man who might be up to no good. Leaving the door open and the Jeep running, she walked carefully toward the car. A man was attempting to meet her halfway, walking slowly, his feet unsteady beneath him.

"Thank God you happened by," he said. Though he wore a heavy coat and a hat, his teeth were already chattering.

Keri took another step and, as she did, lost her footing. She struggled to stay upright, but felt herself falling despite her best efforts. The stranger grabbed on to her, the momentum slamming them both onto the road. Her mind fought to process the rapidly changing events as she caught a good look at his full face. She gasped.

"Are you okay?" he asked, sitting up.

If she hadn't already been on the ground, Keri knew her legs wouldn't have held her up, anyway. Her stomach turned over unpleasantly.

Justin.

Even with a five o'clock shadow, his face was unmistakable. The good-looking teenager she'd loved so long ago had turned into a gorgeous man.

He attempted to stand and crashed back to the ground. "Cowboy boots!" He gave a disgusted grunt.

She wanted to throw herself into his arms, tell him how wonderful it was to see him again, demand an explanation why he had never come back for her. But reason and maturity prevailed. What if he was running from the law? Had he been charged?

Knowing she had to be on her feet first if she was going to gain the upper hand, Keri crawled to her knees and inched to a standing position. She reached behind her and pulled out her pistol. "Hold it," she commanded in her best I'm-a-cop tone of voice. "Turn around and put your hands behind your head."

"You've got to be kidding me."

"Make one wrong move and you'll find out how serious I am," she dared, her heart sliding into her throat. What would she do if he turned violent? If he gained the upper hand out here in the middle of nowhere in blizzard-like conditions.

"Okay, just take it easy. My wallet is in my back pocket. You can have the money. Just…don't get nervous with your trigger finger."

Keri blinked. He thought *she* was the criminal here? "No. I'm…" What *was* she doing? As far as she knew, he hadn't yet been charged. Still…why would he be up here in the winter unless he was running from something? "I'm a cop," she blurted.

He glanced over his shoulder. "You can't arrest me. Last I heard there's no law against sliding off the road."

"I—I know who you are—and about your wife."

Dropping his hands to his side, he turned with a scowl.

Keri adjusted her position, praying that she wouldn't lose her footing.

"I don't know what you saw on the news, lady, but I'm bringing my boys for a vacation."

"Up here? In the winter? That seems a little suspicious to me."

"Look, I don't really care what looks suspicious to you. I'm not running away. I'm free to go wherever I want."

"Oh, yeah? Well, until I have a little chat with my chief and verify that, I'm going to have to detain you."

"How do you plan to do that?"

Was that a challenge? She sent him her fiercest frown. "Any way I have to, tough guy."

He smirked at her bravado. "I meant, how do you plan to get back to town in this ice? You know, for that 'little chat with the chief'?"

Her cheeks warmed, but she refused to give him the satisfaction of knowing he'd rattled her. Instead, she tossed him a glare icier than the pellets stinging her eyelids. "I'm driving a Jeep, if you hadn't noticed. As in four-wheel drive."

He gained his footing and faced her, all traces of amusement gone, his voice steely. "Jeep or no, you're not taking my boys out on the highway in that ice."

"Boys?"

"Yes, my sons. They're in the car."

Keri followed his gaze and saw two identical faces pressed against the window. "You have sons," she said staring back at him.

"Yes, I do. I happen to know there's a cabin down this road where we can go to get my boys out of this weather."

"Nice to know your memory works fine when you're in trouble," she muttered.

"What?"

"Nothing. Get your boys and hop in the Jeep. We'll go to the cabin for the night. And just for your information, I meant I'll have to use the radio and call my chief to see if there's been a warrant issued for your arrest."

He sat back down on the road.

"What are you doing?" Had Justin somehow lost his mind? Was that why he'd never come back? Was this why he'd killed his wife? He was a raving lunatic? Or was he just organizing a one-man sit-in on an icy road in the middle of nowhere, protesting the injustice of getting caught?

Without answering her, he pulled off his boots, stood, and shoved them at her. "I'll have to carry the boys one at a time. I don't want to take a chance on falling and hurting one of them. Hang on to these for me, will you?"

Keri's heart pounded against her ribs as she took the boots and backed up toward the Jeep, tucking her gun in her belt behind her back. Once inside the Jeep, she reached over and unlocked the passenger-side doors— front and back.

In moments, Justin opened the back door and deposited a boy onto the seat. "Scoot over so I can get Billy in," Justin said.

The boy complied. Keri turned in her seat so she could look at him. "What's your name?"

"I'm not supposed to talk to strangers."

Her heart lifted with amusement. "Yeah. You'd think a cop would know that, huh?"

"You're a cop?"

"Yeah."

He sneered. "I don't much like cops."

"All cops or just certain ones?"

A shrug lifted his shoulders through his gray, down-filled jacket. "I don't know. All of them, I guess."

"Most people like me once they get to know me." She sent her best grin to the back of the Jeep. "How about giving me a chance? Looks like we're going to be holed up together for a day or two."

"We will?"

"Yeah. The roads are pretty slick. Your dad thinks we better hang out at my cabin until it's safe to drive."

"Okay." His eyes lit with a glimmer of interest, belying his nonchalant response.

Keri grinned. "So, think we know each other well enough to exchange names?"

"I guess so." He extended his hand. "Josh Kramer."

A lump formed in her throat as she grasped the chubby mittened hand. "Nice to meet you, Josh."

"What's your name?"

"Keri."

"Keri what?"

From the corner of her eye, Keri saw Justin return to the Jeep. At his sharp intake of breath, she knew he'd heard her identify herself. He gently set the second twin in the seat.

His gaze captured hers, accusing her.

Indignation flamed through her like a ball of fire. He, of all people, had the audacity to pretend *she* had betrayed *him?*

"Keri Mahoney?"

"Yes," she said. What else was there to say? Especially in the presence of his sons, whose eyes were wide with curiosity.

"So you're a cop now?"

"That's right. You want to get inside before we freeze?" Her voice remained surprisingly calm, despite the nervous energy pricking her gut like a million needles. "This ice isn't letting up."

"Hang on. I have some groceries in the car." He returned with two bags, deposited them into the back with the boys, then climbed into the front seat. His nearness caused Keri's pulse to race. She passed him his boots. "Better put these back on. You'll be lucky if you don't have frostbite."

"Frostbite is the least of my worries right now." His teeth chattered, and he shivered as he slipped the boots back on.

"Hang on a sec." She switched off the ignition and opened the door.

"What are you doing?"

"You'll see. I'll be right back." Grabbing the keys—just to be on the safe side—Keri hurried to the back of the Jeep, lifted the hatch and pulled out a thick wool blanket…part of the "emergency pack" Dad insisted she keep with her at all times. Now she was glad for his tendency to meddle.

Sliding back under the wheel, she tossed Justin the blanket. "Here. This should help until we get you inside."

"That was thoughtful," he said softly. "Thank you." He unfolded the blanket and brought it up to his neck. And still he shivered. "A warm fire is going to feel great."

"Dad's already at the cabin. I imagine he's got a fire going and a big pot of chili on the stove for tonight's supper. Sound good to you boys?"

"Yeah!" Billy enthused.

"I hate chili." Josh groused.

"Don't be impolite, Josh," Justin admonished.

Billy cast his brother a look of disgust. "Besides, you do so like chili."

The Jeep crawled forward. Tension blanketed the air between Keri and Justin. Unanswered questions, unresolved feelings. Neither spoke until at last Keri parked the vehicle in front of the cabin.

"It looks exactly the same."

She rolled her eyes. "Don't tell Dad. He spent all summer and way more of his retirement fund than necessary getting it fixed up. This is our first vacation up here since… In a long time."

"Really?" He turned to look at her. "I've always pictured you here every summer. Like when we were kids."

"You've thought of me?" As soon as the words flew out of her mouth, Keri wished she could snatch them back. She cringed. It wouldn't do to show him she still cared. Not only was it pathetic, given the fact that he'd obviously moved on without her, but they might very well be on opposite sides of the law right now, and no matter how "cowboyish" that sounded, it was the simple truth.

"Are we going in?" The irritation in Josh's voice jarred her to action.

"Of course."

She reached for the door but stopped at the pressure of Justin's hand on her arm.

"Wait a sec," he whispered. He raised his voice to address his sons. "Boys, go on up to the porch. But be careful."

When they were out of the Jeep and on their way to the porch, Justin turned to her. "Keri, I want you to know that I'm innocent."

Keri snorted, trying hard not to be taken in by his beautiful, soulful eyes. "Prisons are full of innocent men."

His brows narrowed. "Listen, I didn't kill my wife. But whether you believe me or not doesn't make any difference. I just wanted you to know that you don't have to be nervous about me staying at the cabin."

Keri sobered and focused her attention on the boys, who were stomping and waving for them to hurry up. She swallowed hard. "I'm not scared." Confused, hurt, angry. Why hadn't he come back as he'd promised? Why had he left and never once written to her?

She gripped the wheel and kept her eyes forward, but she could feel Justin studying her. She couldn't speak. If she tried, she'd make a complete fool of herself by demanding answers.

Finally, he drew a breath. "All right. There's nothing we can do tonight. No one's going anywhere in this weather. As far as I know they haven't issued a warrant yet, but if you find out that they have, I'll let you take me in."

She nodded. "Fair enough."

He gave her a sad smile and covered her hand with his. "It's good to see you again."

He opened the car door and went to join the twins.

Switching on the radio, Keri tried to raise the chief. She could put an end to all this right now.

"This is Deputy Mahoney. You there, Chief? Over."

Dead silence.

She gave it a few more tries then sighed in frustration. That dumb Abe. She'd have to try again later, after the chief figured out the radio had been switched off.

She glanced at the porch where Justin and the boys waited. In all of her years of dreaming of Justin, Keri had never imagined emotions as intense as the ones invading her heart at that moment. She closed her eyes and gathered a deep breath. She had to keep her head on straight. This Justin wasn't the same one she'd known. But try as she might to convince herself of that, her heart had a mind of its own.

Fifteen years notwithstanding, she still loved Justin Kramer.

He had to find the tape. Even if it meant sacrificing Justin and the twins to get it, he wouldn't go to jail. He couldn't.

The vinyl weight bench stuck to his bare back as he pushed the barbell up.

Breathe in, bring the weight down. Breathe out, push it back up. In…out. In…out. For the first time in his life, he felt as if he was in over his head. The whole situation was driving him nuts, and his stomach burned all the time—enough to keep the antacid companies in business. Ironically, all those nerves had given him the push he needed to get in the best workout he'd had in a month.

His gut clenched again. He had to find that videotape before anyone else did.

Breathing heavily, he sat up on the weight bench and grabbed his water bottle off the floor next to him. The tepid liquid soothed his dry throat, but nothing could soothe the anxiety gripping him night and day like a vise. Sweat trickled down his back. Amelia should never have tried to force his hand. Slamming the bottle to the floor, he lay back on the bench.

In…out. In…out.

* * *

Memories assaulted Justin as he stepped inside the cabin. Memories of tanned legs and dripping wet hair from summers spent swimming in the creek with Keri. As close as their two families had been for the first fourteen years of their lives, Justin could well imagine he and Keri might have ended up married, continuing those summer traditions into the next generation. If only things hadn't unraveled that summer his parents died. Regret slashed across his heart at the possibility of what might have been.

Keri's voice brought him back to reality. "Dad, you remember Justin Kramer, don't you?" She sounded as carefree as if she didn't suspect him of murder.

The joy brightening Mac Mahoney's lined face was unmistakable and warmed Justin more than the roaring fire in the fireplace. "What kind of a question is that? Of course I remember him." Tears glistened in faded green eyes as the grizzled older man wrapped his arms around Justin. "It's good to see you, boy. Good to see you. Been too long."

"Yes it has." When Mr. Mahoney turned him loose, Justin reached for the twins. "I'd like you to meet my sons, Billy and Josh."

Mac smiled and winked. "No one would ever guess you two are related."

Billy returned his grin.

Josh sneered. "Like we've never heard that one before."

"Josh!" Justin scowled. "You owe Mr. Mahoney an apology."

The boy shrugged. "Sorry." But his face didn't reflect remorse.

"I'm sorry. Josh and Billy lost their mother recently. These last few months have been difficult."

Keri's dad waved aside the apology, his eyes alight with sympathy. "Don't worry about it. I was just about to whip up a batch of my famous donuts." He cut a glance at the boys. "Anyone interested in helping me out?"

Billy's face lit with a wide grin. "Yes, sir!"

Mac smiled back, then focused on Josh. "How about you?"

The boy's eyes showed interest, but in an obvious attempt to maintain his churlish manner, he shrugged again. "I guess."

Justin held his grin in check.

"Great!" Mac rubbed his hands together. "Keri can show you where to put your coats. Come into the kitchen after your hands are washed."

"Follow me, gents," Keri said and walked toward the bedroom.

As soon as the boys were out of the room, Mac eyed Justin, studying his face as though trying to put his finger on the situation. "What brings you to our neck of the woods?"

Though his body had aged and his shoulders had stooped a bit over the past fifteen years, Keri's dad appeared to have retained the instincts that had caused him to hold the position of Briarwood's chief of police for as long as Justin could remember.

"The boys and I just needed to get away for a while. I hope you don't mind me just showing up. I didn't think anyone would be here." As soon as he spoke the last words, his face warmed. If Mac and Keri hadn't been here, he'd have been breaking and entering.

Mac seemed to ignore that, still he peered closer. "You bringing trouble with you?" Mac squinted, his eyes demanding the truth.

"I don't think so."

Keri's dad nodded, but his expression remained stoic. "Does this 'need to get away' have anything to do with your wife's death? Raven works for a TV station in Kansas City. She called us when it first happened."

"Yes. I found her...in our house."

He arched a wooly gray eyebrow. "You guilty?"

"No, sir."

He would have liked to explain. To make Mr. Mahoney believe that he was still the same boy he'd treated as his own son all those years ago. That he wasn't capable of such a crime. But voices carried back into the room, signaling Keri and the boys' return.

Mac gave him another studied look. "We'll talk about it later." He headed for the kitchen without waiting for Justin's response. "Follow me, boys. I got sidetracked catching up with your dad, so you can help me grab the ingredients out of the cabinets."

The boys followed, their quick easy steps indicative of their relief to be in a lighter atmosphere. Guilt shrouded Justin, and for the first time he found himself second-guessing his decision to leave town. Innocent men were found innocent in most cases. What would happen if a warrant had already been issued for his arrest and Keri Mahoney of all people had to take him in? A throat clearing caught his attention, and he jerked his gaze from the kitchen door to Keri.

She motioned for him to take a seat on the rustic, woodsy-printed couch.

"Thanks." He walked into the sitting area and dropped into cushions, running his hand over the stubble covering his jaw.

Keri shed her jacket and tossed it across the arm of the chair next to the fireplace. Silence loomed, a thick black cloud of tension, as she wordlessly grabbed the poker and pushed at the glowing logs. Justin watched the sparks shoot up the chimney. She tossed another log into place, situated it just right, then replaced the poker on the stand. She turned to face him.

As their eyes met, memories rushed back to him on a wave of yesterday's dreams. This was the girl he'd loved for the first fourteen years of his life. The one he very well might have married if things hadn't gotten so fouled up.

The way she stared at him, he could imagine she was having similar thoughts. She cleared her throat. "So…"

"Listen. I don't expect to talk about the good old days." Justin gave her a lopsided grin.

"Good. It's probably better for us both to keep our past friendship out of this whole situation." With a heavy sigh, she plopped into the chair next to the fire and kicked her legs up to the ottoman.

"I didn't do it." Suddenly, it became very important that Keri believe him. And whether they discussed the past or not, it was there…simmering on the edge of both of their minds. If she remembered him at all, she just couldn't believe that he'd take a life.

"Look, Justin. It's not my job to determine whether

you're guilty or not. It's my job to take you in if a warrant has been issued. If your boys weren't with you, I'd handcuff you to something to make sure you don't run. I'm trusting your integrity to keep you here."

"I already told you. I'll let you arrest me if you have to."

A spark of the Keri he remembered returned in the stubborn jerk of her chin. She leveled a stern gaze at him. "I don't need you to *let* me take you anywhere. I'm a trained officer of the law and if I say you're going in, you are."

Justin's eyes flickered over her petite frame and he couldn't resist the grin tipping the corners of his lips.

Anger sparked Keri's eyes. She shot to her feet and leaned over him, filling the air between them with the combined scents of peach-scented soap and wood smoke. "Listen, Kramer, don't test me. I don't want to cuff you unless it's absolutely necessary, but I will if you force my hand."

He could see she was dead serious, and it only struck him funnier. Laughter started low in his throat and, try as he might, there was no stopping it.

Red splotches appeared on her neck and freckled face, and sparks shot from her green eyes. "Stop laughing!"

"I'm sorry," he said, fighting for air. "You're just… so cute."

"That does it."

Before Justin could contain his mirth and take charge of the situation, Keri sprang into action, twisted his arm to the side and slapped the cuffs on one wrist. In practically one motion, he found himself with one hand cuffed to the wooden arm of the couch. Keri stood over him, breathing heavily, but smug with victory. Her hands rested on her slim hips, and she raised her brows, her green eyes daring him to laugh now.

Anger bit into him like a vice. "All right," he ground out, "you've made your point. Let me go."

Her shoulders rose and fell with an exaggerated sigh. "You know what? I've been up for more than twenty-four hours. I went to work early yesterday because a drunk wrapped his truck around a telephone pole and nearly killed a group of kids. I sat listening to that same drunk whine about his rights all night while I tried to get paperwork done." She stretched, then covered a wide yawn. "Then just when I was about to head out and start a much-needed vacation, I find you on Krahoney Road—suspiciously, I might add. So I think I'm within my rights to handcuff you until I know if you're running from an arrest warrant."

"Well, I'm sorry to add to your stress," he drawled, "but I'm the one they're accusing of murder." He scowled. "Wrongfully!"

"Maybe. Maybe not."

"Let me go, Keri. I don't want the boys to see me like this."

"You know my dad will make dozens and dozens of donuts and donut holes. Your boys will be glazing for hours." Keri grabbed a crocheted afghan from the chair and tossed it over his arm, concealing the metal constraints. "Perfect. I'm going to go and shower, then I'll probably take a nice long nap. If you behave yourself, I might release you when I get back." She threw him a victorious grin and sauntered away, leaving him scowling after her.

"You know, you're stomping all over my civil rights! I could sue you!"

"Go ahead," she called over her shoulder. "The line forms behind Junior Connor."

Whatever that meant. Defeated, he twisted around and swung his legs over the side of the couch. It felt good to stretch out after several tension-filled hours in the car. He adjusted the afghan so that it covered his arm and shoulder, then spread it over the rest of him. Relaxing in the toasty warmth of a wood fire, Justin closed his eyes. He felt his chest rising and falling in slow even breaths just before he drifted away into the precious comfort of sleep.

Keri leaned into the shower's spray, resting her hands flat against the tiled wall. She winced. Partly from the blast of hot water and partly from the memory of her encounter with Justin. She'd taken him completely by surprise, but what if he'd been ready for her? Would she have been able to take him?

The thought frustrated her and filled her with self-doubt. What kind of chief of police would she make if she couldn't even arrest a prisoner just because he had ten inches on her and a good fifty pounds?

And blue eyes to die for.

Still…despite the same charming grin and sincere eyes, she didn't really know him anymore. He might be anything. Even…well…a murderer.

The problem was that her heart didn't want to believe it. She wanted to believe that the devastatingly good-looking man of her dreams, who seemed to be a wonderful father to boot, was everything she remembered. And more. The dismal reality was that he could quite possibly be a sociopath who'd murdered his wife, felt no remorse, and could probably pass ten lie-detector tests, all the while planning his next murder.

She shuddered, even as her heart rejected the notion.

The water went from too hot to freezing by the time she soaped up, rinsed off, washed her hair and grabbed a towel. Shivering, she dried off and dressed in comfy sweats and headed for the door. When she stepped into the hall, the aroma of fried donuts drifted between the wooden walls, beckoning her toward the kitchen. Try as she might, she couldn't keep herself from peeking at Justin as she walked through. He was stretched out on the couch, the afghan discreetly covering the handcuffs.

A lump formed in her throat at the sight of him, sleeping peacefully, like a man with nothing to hide. She snorted and turned. Or a sociopath with no conscience!

Willing away thoughts of Justin, she pushed through the kitchen door and stopped short at the sight of the two boys working diligently to glaze a batch of cooled donuts while her dad stood, back to them, lifting more from the boiling grease.

Billy popped a donut hole into his mouth, licked his fingers, then glanced up. His guilt-clouded eyes widened when they lit on Keri. Silently, she lifted her brow, attempting a stern expression of reprimand. He held out a donut, hung by one sticky finger, and pressed the other index finger to his lips.

An obvious attempt to buy her silence.

Pretending to consider the proposition, Keri rested her hands on her hips for a second, then she looked him square in the eye, winked and nodded. She reached for the goodie. Hesitating only a moment at the thought of how many times the kid must have licked his fingers without being caught, she nevertheless took a bite.

"What are you doing, Keri-girl?"

Keri jumped at her dad's voice and she stopped chewing, hiding the rest of the donut behind her back.

"What kind of example is that setting for the boys?" he demanded. "Stealing donuts right out from under my nose?" The twinkle·in his eyes belied his tone, but Keri played along for the twins' entertainment.

"You're right, Dad," she said solemnly. She set the donut on a napkin and headed for the fridge. "I've set a horrible example, and I'm sorry. How could I ever have taken a bite of this delicious donut... without first dunking it in milk?" She held up the gallon jug and the boys giggled. She set it on the counter, grabbed four glasses and began to pour.

Mac Mahoney grinned and winked at Josh and Billy. "You boys about ready to sample our cooking?"

"Yes, sir!"

"Alrighty, then." He laid a napkin in front of each of them, next to their milk. "Grab a donut from the plate and let's start sampling!"

Keri finished her donut and milk, enjoying the ecstasy on the boys' faces. Billy delighted in everything, from the blarney Dad told of leprechauns and four-leaf clovers, to the simple task of throwing away his napkin and carefully placing his empty glass into the sink. Josh, too, seemed to enjoy the atmosphere, offering half smiles and short replies. But the joy that seemed to exude from Billy was noticeably absent from Josh's demeanor.

When the boys were done with their snack, the three

guys started on another batch of donuts. Keri excused herself.

Her glance returned once more to Justin, sleeping on the couch. With a sigh, she headed back to her bedroom, snatched her keys from the dresser and tiptoed close to Justin. She knelt beside the couch. He groaned and shifted, causing her heart nearly to stop. Watching him as he settled back into sleep, her heart picked up. A lock of his hair fell across his forehead, begging her to smooth it back. Obeying the summons, she reached forward.

His eyes opened and Keri thought she'd die.

"What are you doing?" he whispered.

Heat seared her cheeks. "I—I was going to uncuff you."

"Really?"

She nodded. "I'm counting on your word to keep you here."

In a swift movement, she slipped the key into the cool metal cuffs and set him free.

He sat up, rubbing his wrist. "Thanks." His hand reached out and gently cupped her cheek. The pool of emotion reflected in his eyes was too deep for Keri's comfort.

She shot to her feet, plopped her hands on her hips, and hardened her heart. "Just don't give me a reason to regret it."

He'd been pacing this same stretch of floor off and on for the past two hours. Why hadn't Justin called? He'd had plenty of time to get settled into wherever he was headed.

First thing he would do when Justin finally made contact was weasel the location of his hideout.

Releasing a chuckle, he shook his head at his own brilliance. Justin's absence made the chump look even guiltier than the eyewitness stories. The D.A. would almost certainly seek a warrant now.

He would have liked to have come up with more credible witnesses than a couple of bums who would sell out their own mothers to get enough money for a bottle of cheap whisky and enough coke for one high. But he hadn't dared try to pay off anyone who was sober. As long as they kept to the story, he'd buy all the whisky they could drink. If they didn't keep to the story…well…he'd made it pretty clear that killing a couple of bums wouldn't hurt his conscience any more than putting a bullet in that tramp's head had.

Once he found out where Justin was staying, he would send the cops an anonymous tip. Then he would be the most supportive of Justin's friends. Insisting upon his innocence. Hey, he might even offer to raise the twins. He smiled, imagining the light in his wife's eyes when he presented her with the children she'd always longed for. Yes, Justin's boys would work just as well as going through an agency. This plan just grew sweeter by the second. Now all he had to do was wait for Justin to call.

He stopped pacing for a second and stared at the phone. "Ring!"

Chapter Four

Insistent ringing woke Justin from a dream world in which he was fourteen years old again, free, unfettered and loving Keri Mahoney. Where no murder was hanging over his head, and his little boys weren't in jeopardy of losing their only security. Being awakened from such a dream did nothing to lighten his first mood of the day. "All right, already," he groused. "Hold on a second."

Justin reached toward the nightstand. Fumbling for the cordless, he squinted as his eyes protested the lighted room. His hand connected with an unfamiliar cell phone.

"Hello?"

"Mac?" a woman's Southern drawl asked.

"No, this is Justin."

"Where's Mac?"

It took a second for his muddled brain to register where he was—Mac Mahoney had insisted Justin and the twins take his room. Before he had the chance to reply, the woman's voice rose in pitch and volume. "If you did one little thing to hurt him, I'll—"

Raking a hand through his hair, Justin felt panic rise. All he needed was someone else accusing him of a crime. "Wait, lady. Calm down. Mr. Mahoney is fine. Hang on a sec, and I'll go get him."

Justin headed for the door and stepped into the hallway, coming face-to-face with Keri. She looked adorable with tousled auburn hair caressing her face and pillow imprints lining her cheek.

"I heard a phone ring," she said, her sleep-husky voice doing crazy things to his heart. "Did you bring a cell?"

"Yes, but it's in the car. This one is for your dad." He extended the phone to her.

Outrage branded her face, and she snatched the device from his hand. "Dad! You promised you weren't going to bring a phone! We're supposed to be getting away from it all!"

Justin stared after Keri as she stomped barefoot into the living room. Mac came out of the kitchen, wiping his hands on a towel. Justin caught a whiff of bacon frying and his stomach rumbled in appreciation.

"What's the yelling about?" Mr. Mahoney demanded. "You're going to wake up the whole house!"

"Phone for you." Keri gave him an accusing glare and handed over the phone in a jerky I-don't-like-this-one-bit motion.

"It must be Ruth. I couldn't go a whole week without talking to my Ruthie." Mac's lips tilted into a sheepish grin and he shrugged as he took the phone. "Hi, doll," he said into the receiver. "What? Oh, that was Keri. Who'd you think it was? A man answered?" Justin grinned and waved. "Oh, him... Old friend of the family. He's spending a few days up here with his twin boys. You should see those kids. Like two peas in a pod, they are. Can't tell 'em apart until you get to know 'em a bit."

Mac darted a glance to include first Justin, then Keri. "Wait just a second, hon." He put his hand over the mouthpiece. "I'm going to take this into the kitchen."

"By all means," Keri said with a huff and a dismissive wave. "You might as well, now. Just tell her not to spill the beans about us having a phone up here or Manning will try and weasel me back to work. He's probably been swamped with calls since this ice storm hit."

Mac sent her a scowl and headed into the kitchen.

Amusement worked through Justin, but fell short of reaching his lips as he realized that the only reason Mac had a girlfriend was because Keri's mother had died. A fact he had discovered during his earlier conversation with Mr. Mahoney.

He reached out and touched her shoulder. "Keri, your dad told me what happened to your mom. I'm sorry."

Keri swung around to face him, her face suddenly void of color. "Don't pretend you didn't know," she said, as though not quite able to catch enough breath to give the words full volume. "I wrote to you at your aunt's house when it happened. I begged you to come to the funeral."

Justin felt as though he'd been sucker punched. Keri had needed him, and he hadn't been there for her? He couldn't resist putting his finger to the slight pucker of her chin as she fought to control tears. "I promise I never got a letter from you. If one came to us, it never made it into my hands."

She eyed him as if scrutinizing his words. "Your aunt sent flowers. I still have the card at home, somewhere. It was signed... Please accept our condolences for your loss. Toni and Justin."

"Toni must have read my mail and sent the flowers. She never told me about it. I'd have come right away if I'd known."

Her eyes misted. "You stopped writing to me after four measly letters. I just figured you didn't care."

"I would have cared if I had known." Justin moved his hand to cup her cheek. "I do care. I loved her like a second mom, remember?"

Suddenly the expression on Keri's face became stony. She jerked away. "I remember a lot of things that you've obviously forgotten."

Justin dropped his hand to his side and followed her into the living room. He wanted to reassure her. To excuse himself of the broken promises. But he had no acceptable excuses to offer. And the truth was too sad to share: that it hadn't taken long, in a Godless environment, for him to begin questioning his faith. It had only taken a little while longer before the doubts combined with temptations, until soon he didn't even recognize himself.

Keri's slender hands trembled as she grabbed the fireplace poker. And despite the fact that she was holding a potential weapon, Justin pressed the conversation forward.

"I remember everything. Probably better than you do, Keri. But things changed when I went to live with

Aunt Toni. Kids tend to change, you know? My whole world upended. How can you hold a grudge against a fourteen-year-old boy?"

She spun around and brandished the poker like a sword, her face filled with outrage. "A grudge? What kind of egomaniac are you to think that I'm still carrying a torch for you?"

Avoiding the couch, Justin did a quick examination of the recliner next the fireplace. The print was identical to the couch, but the arms were fat and cushiony. No chance of being handcuffed to that thing. He sat, eyeing her carefully. "I didn't say anything about a torch. I said a grudge."

The thunder left her suddenly red face, and she turned back to building a fire. "Yeah, well, I'm not carrying one of those, either."

She pushed at the coals, trying to stir them up, then gave a frustrated growl as the fireplace remained lifeless, except for a few glowing embers.

"Do you want me to do that?"

A short laugh escaped her and she shot him a twisted grin. "When was the last time you built a fire?"

He returned her grin and nodded. "The winter before I moved to Kansas City."

"Thanks for the offer. But I think it'll get done a little quicker if I do it myself."

"Breakfast is ready." Justin and Keri both turned at the sound of Mr. Mahoney's announcement. The older man's bushy brows pushed together. "Where are the boys?"

Justin smiled. "They're not up yet."

The old man looked crestfallen. "Made 'em some of

my special cinnamon hot chocolate," he mumbled. "Josh likes bacon. It's bound to get cold."

"I'll go get them up." Justin started toward the bedroom he shared with his sons, then stopped as an idea struck him. "Mr. Mahoney, can I borrow your phone for just a few minutes?"

"No!" Keri shot up from her crouched position in front of the fireplace. Her eyes sparked with fierce determination. "We are not giving you access to phone an accomplice." She padded through the living room and to the empty space of room between the hall and the kitchen door.

"For crying out loud, at least let him explain." Mr. Mahoney sent her a scowl, then turned his focus to Justin. "Who'd you want to call?"

"I just want to check in with my boss at the Mission. There are a couple of the residents I've been counseling who I feel are about ready to make a commitment to Christ. I want to let Rick know to follow up with them. Plus I've been in charge of the Thanksgiving dinner at the mission for several years and I won't be there to take care of things. He needs to be aware of that."

"Well, now. That sounds reasonable to me."

Folding her arms, Keri looked like a petulant child. "It doesn't to me," she insisted.

Justin fought back his grin for fear she'd take him by surprise and handcuff him again, if he gave in to his amusement.

"The phone isn't yours, Keri-girl," Mac shot back. "So it's not your decision, anyhow."

Keri's eyes blazed. Justin could see she was attempt-

ing to maintain her composure and her respectful attitude for her dad. He had to admire that, given the circumstances. She directed her argument to her dad as
though Justin wasn't even there.

"For all we know, Justin is a murderer. Giving him
a haven from the ice and snow is one thing, but do we
really have to let him use the phone? We don't know if
he's planning to call an accomplice. If I had one shred
of proof, I'd cuff him to a pole until all this blows over."

Mac snorted. "You're just wanting to show your
muscles. Even prisoners are allowed one phone call.
Besides, for all you know Justin's been cleared of the
crime by now. Innocent until proven guilty. Remember?"

A scowl marred Keri's face. She looked at Justin
then back to her dad before Justin had a chance to work
a smile on her.

She planted her hands on her hips. "All right, he can
use the phone. For five minutes." She focused her gaze
upon Justin. "But I listen to every word you say."

Mac opened his mouth as though he was about to
protest, but Justin spoke up quickly before the two Irish
heads butted over him. "That's fine with me. I have
nothing to hide."

"All right. Then it's all settled." Mac tossed Justin
the phone and rubbed his hands together. "How about
some breakfast first?" He glanced past Justin and his
face brightened. "Well, good morning, lads. We thought
you were going to sleep the day away."

"We smelled bacon." A wide yawn stretched Billy's
pink mouth.

"That you did. That you did. Follow me and I'll get

you some while it's still warm." He sent both boys a wink. "And I have hot chocolate for you. With a special ingredient."

"What special ingredient?" Billy asked, his voice rising in wonder.

"You'll have to see if you can guess."

Both sets of eyes went wide, and the twins glanced at Justin for permission—Billy with eager anticipation, Josh with mildly piqued interest. "We washed our hands," Josh said.

Justin smiled at his sons. Though the boys had gotten themselves dressed, both blond heads needed a wet-down and a combing. But he figured that could wait. No use in them eating a cold meal. "I'm starving. Let's go eat."

"I have to finish the fire. Save me a couple slices of bacon, will you Dad?"

Mac leveled a gaze at her. "You're not going to eat with the rest of us?"

"No, I need to get this going."

"You know, maybe you better save me some breakfast, too," Justin said. "I think I'll help Keri with the fire."

"Fine," Mack grumbled. "Josh and Billy and me can manage on our own, can't we, boys? Let those two eat a cold breakfast. What do we care?" He ushered the boys into the kitchen, leaving Justin alone with Keri.

She eyed him dubiously. "I told you I don't need your help to get the fire going. It's just taking a bit longer because the coals are practically gone."

"I thought I might go ahead and call Rick while the boys are occupied."

Keri nodded. "Good idea."

Justin reclaimed his seat in the recliner and dialed the number to the mission. Rick answered on the fourth ring, sounding breathless.

"Rick?"

Silence.

"Hello?"

"Hang on a sec."

Justin heard the receiver clunk down on the desk. Rick returned quickly. "I closed the door. Never know who's listening in. Are you and the boys okay? I've been calling your house and cell like crazy. Where are you?"

"We're fine. Just took the boys on a little vacation over Thanksgiving."

Rick hesitated. "I see. How long will you be gone?"

"I'm not sure. I need to ask you about something the police mentioned yesterday."

"What's that?"

"They say two eyewitnesses have come forward. Men who stayed at the mission and have signed sworn affidavits that I left in the night."

"That's not possible."

"The police seem to think it is."

"What I mean to say is that I don't think they're men from our mission. I think someone is paying a couple of guys off to pretend they stayed here and to say they saw you."

"What about the register?"

"That would be easy enough to fake with all the guys in and out of here for one night only."

"True."

"Can you tell me where you are?" Rick's hushed voice was tense with concern. "I hate the thought of you and the boys hiding out."

A chuckle escaped him. "I told you. It's just a vacation. We're not hiding out. As a matter of fact. We're at a cabin a few hours away from Kansas City."

"A cabin…in the winter? In Missouri?"

"It's a long story. Anyway, make sure you check up on Gary and Brian will you? I think they're both pretty close to receiving Christ. I don't want this problem of mine to jeopardize that."

"Sure, I'll check up on them. Call again soon, and let me know you're still okay. Is there anything I can do for you on this end?"

"Yeah. Listen, this phone's losing steam fast. I need to charge it. Can you call Bob and let him know I'll be back in a few days?"

"Sure, anything else?"

"Just pray, will you?"

After giving him Bob's number, Justin hung up, feeling heavier somehow than he had before. He glanced up to find Keri standing over him with her hand open and waiting.

He handed over the phone and leaned back in the chair, closing his eyes. "Satisfied that I wasn't speaking with an accomplice?"

"Sure," she muttered. "I hope you're enjoying your vacation, because so far mine stinks."

"Oh, yeah. It's just a carnival ride a second." Releasing a weary sigh, Justin opened his eyes to look at her. "You're really self-absorbed, aren't you? I didn't remember that about you. Or is it something new?"

She gasped, then recovered enough for anger to take over, evidenced in her sparking eyes as she dropped the poker and leaned over his chair, one hand resting on either armrest. Her face was inches from his. "Let me tell you something, Justin Kramer. As far as I'm concerned, you're a suspect, possibly on the run from the law. Nothing else. Now it looks like the ice has stopped, so I'd imagine by tomorrow, the salt trucks will make it onto this highway. You'll be on your way, and I'll forget I ever knew you. Don't use our memories to try to get to me. Like you said. Kids change."

"Nothing more than a suspect on the run, eh? I mean nothing to you?"

"That's right, Buster!"

Justin cupped the back of her neck and brought her closer, until their breaths mingled. "Then why are there tears in your eyes?" he whispered.

Her lips trembled, drawing his attention. Warning bells sounded in his head, but he ignored them as her eyes widened and her lips parted in a sudden intake of breath. Pulling her closer, he closed his eyes, ready to lose himself in Keri's arms and the sweetness of her kiss.

Pain exploded in his cheek. His eyes shot open. "Hey!" He turned her loose and cupped his own face.

She straightened up. Her chest heaved, and she glared down at him. "Listen, Bucko. For someone who didn't kill his wife, you're awfully quick to put her out of your mind and cozy up to another woman."

Outrage filled Justin at the accusation. "You don't know anything about my relationship—"

"You know what? I don't care. It's not my problem.

If you try anything like that again, I'll handcuff you until it's time to take you in—even if I have to wait until you're asleep and handcuff you to Dad's bed."

Fire flamed in her eyes, warning him off. He sat back, bewilderment washing over him. Where was the Keri he'd left behind? The sweet kid who—well, not to be conceited, or anything, but who had hung on his every word?

She grabbed her coat and threw it on over her sweatshirt, snatched up a pair of rubber boots, and pulled a stocking cap from the coat pocket. "Go eat breakfast, Justin. And don't forget what I said."

Keri stomped onto the porch, underestimated the ice beneath her, and fought to maintain her footing. Only a last-ditch grapple for the railing kept her from landing hard on her behind. But that near-catastrophe was nothing compared to what had almost happened inside the cabin. Her lips tingled, whether from the almost kiss, or the chill in the air, she didn't know. Nor did she want to know. How dare Justin have the gall to think she still loved him?

She hadn't meant to be so transparent. Over and over, she reminded herself, this Justin was not the same one who had left Briarwood fifteen years earlier.

With carefully guided steps, she made her way to the Jeep. She grabbed the keys out of her pocket, unlocked the door and slid into the driver's seat. First things first. She cranked the ignition, and the engine roared to life, sending a shot of freezing air through the wide-open vents.

She gasped from the shock of the cold blast rushing into the Jeep. With a flick of her numbed fingers, she closed the vent. Why hadn't she thought to grab gloves? Justin. That's why. He'd rattled her so much, she hadn't followed even the most basic of weather-survival training. Reaching forward she tested the air. Not exactly warm, but better than icy. She switched on the radio. All the emergency vehicles including Ed's road crew trucks were on the same channel, so there was bound to be someone out there listening.

"This is Officer Mahoney. Anyone out there? Over."

"That you Keri, honey? We've been trying to raise you all night. Over."

Keri groaned. What was the chief doing on the radio this time of the morning? Today was supposedly his day off.

"Yeah, Chief," she said with a sigh. "It's me. We're all iced in up here. What's it like in town? Over."

"Bad. We're warning people to stay home, but you know how folks are—everyone thinks they're the only ones who can drive on ice, and every other driver on the road is an idiot. We've had more than a dozen minor accidents since it all started. Over."

"What about the highways? Over," Keri broke in before he could hint around for her to come in and help with traffic calls. He and Abe were more than capable of taking care of a few fender benders without her.

"Now, don't you even think of trying to get out on Highway 13. As it is, it's going to be at least tomorrow afternoon before the crews get out there. But the forecast is calling for six more inches of snow tonight, so they may not get out for another day or two. You and Mac just hold tight and don't worry about anything here in town. Over."

Shame washed over Keri at the chief's concern for her well-being. "All right, Chief. But don't you work too hard. No sense wearing yourself out. Over."

"I'll do my best. Over."

"Uh—Chief, get any faxes from KCPD? Arrest warrants? Anything like that? Over." She knew she was about as subtle as a ticking bomb, but didn't know how to approach the subject any other way.

"Nothing that I know of. Over."

Relief spread calming fingers through her.

"All right. Just wondering. You take it easy and I'll check in again later. Keep Abe away from the switch, will you? Over."

She heard his chuckle. "I'll do that. Enjoy your vacation. Over and out."

Keri switched off the radio. Tucking her hands inside her pockets to get them warm, she leaned back and stared at the icy landscape.

Chapter Five

He drummed his fingers across his sleek desktop and took a long, slow drag from his cigarette. With a satisfying sense of release he watched the smoke billow through the air above him. He knew people in the smoke-free building suspected he lit up in his office, but what did he care? It was his office. And since he locked the door first and opened the window to get rid of the smell, they couldn't actually prove it.

It irked him that a man couldn't smoke where he wanted. So much for living in a free country. Even New York City, of all places, had passed a no-smoking ordinance. Pretty soon even the smallest of pleasures like an after-dinner cigarette would be banned everywhere.

A sudden cough rumbled through his chest. He frowned at the pain shooting through his lungs, then took another drag.

So Justin had made it to some hideout. Somewhere he thought he was safe. Funny thing about feeling safe. Just when you least expect it. WHAM! The hammer falls. Amelia knew that. She'd thought she was pretty smart.

If his wife had found out... Well, he couldn't have let that happen, could he? He might not be the most faithful of husbands, but she was the only woman he'd ever loved. The only one he would ever love. She was the only thing in his life that was good. Everything he'd done had only been for her sake. She didn't know it, but it was only for her sake. And he'd do whatever it took to make sure she was protected from all the ugliness. Whatever it took....

Keri felt great after a Pilates routine in the privacy of her bedroom, a quick shower, and an hour of devotions to make up for wigging out on God the night before.

Peals of laughter carried through the house from the kitchen, causing her to grin into the silence. Unable to resist, she closed her Bible and followed the sound. All four "men" were embroiled in a capture-the-world board game.

"Hi, Keri!" Billy greeted her, his eyes wide with excitement. "My armies just took out one of Dad's."

"*Miss* Keri," Justin gently reminded, ruffling the boy's hair to take the bite out of the scolding.

The little boy seemed unfazed. He gave her a wide grin. "Sorry, Miss Keri."

Keri couldn't hold back her chuckle. "It's all right. How are you doing, Josh?"

The boy scowled and motioned to the board. "My armies are blue."

At the sight of the sparse number of blue armies, she

sent him a sympathetic wink. "Oops. Looks like you've lost a few battles."

"You think so?" His tongue dripped with sarcasm as he gave her a withering look.

Taken aback, Keri was speechless.

"Josh!" Justin's stern voice made her jump. "Apologize to Miss Keri, right now. It's not her fault you're losing the game."

Josh threw the dice across the table and shot to his feet. He glared at her. "I'm not sorry!" Running past her, he disappeared through the kitchen door.

"I'll take care of this," Justin said, his jaw clenched. Keri touched his arm as he walked past. He stopped, towering above her.

"Don't be too hard on him. He has his reasons for behaving this way, and I have a feeling it doesn't have anything to do with the game. At least talk to him before you make him apologize or whatever you intend to do to him."

His expression softened and Keri thought her heart might burst from her chest. He reached forward and trailed his finger along her jawline. "I'll go easy on him."

She looked down to keep from revealing what she knew he already suspected: that despite her doubts about him, the wondering, the agonizing reality of what she had to do, despite all those things, she loved him still. She didn't look back up until Justin disappeared through the kitchen door.

"Well, I guess that pretty much wraps up the game, then doesn't it?"

Though Dad spoke the words to Billy, he kept his scrutinizing gaze fixed on Keri.

Her cheeks burned. "Excuse me," she said. "I have to—" What? What did she have to do? Her mind was blank. She had to escape. To be alone with her thoughts. To make sense of her jumbled emotions. "I'm going to my room."

She left them staring after her. The door to the room Justin was sharing with his boys hung slightly ajar when she walked by on the way to her own sanctuary. Her curiosity got the better of her and she halted her steps and listened.

"I hate him!" Josh's voice leaked through the door.

Peeking inside, Keri saw Justin shift on the bed so that he could put his arms around his son.

"You can't hate the man who killed your mom, Josh. It'll eat you alive. Believe me, I know. You have to learn to forgive. Once the devil weakens you with bitterness, he can lie to you until you don't live for Jesus anymore."

Her stomach flopped. What exactly was Justin saying here? *Believe me, I know.* Was he saying he hated the man who killed his wife? Or was he saying he'd hated his wife and the devil had used it to weaken him to the point that he'd killed her?

Deep in thought, she jumped when Justin appeared at the threshold. So much for her cop instincts. Sheesh.

Confusion showed in his face when he found her outside his door. "Keri? What are you doing?"

She opened her mouth to form a good excuse, but nothing sprang to mind. With a sheepish grin, she shrugged. "Eavesdropping?"

Justin chuckled. "At least you're still honest."

"How's Josh?"

"He fell asleep. How much did you hear?"

"Enough. Still preaching the same old sermons?"

"What do you mean?"

"The 'forgiveness' speech. You know…what you just told Josh. Not that it wasn't good, but it's exactly the same as when we were kids."

His brows lifted. "I didn't realize I had a 'forgiveness speech,' but truth is always truth."

Keri nodded. "You're right, of course." After all, she was the one still serving the Lord, not him.

Justin stepped all the way out of the room and shut the door softly. He leaned back, resting the sole of his shoe on the door, and folded his arms. "What did you mean about this being the same speech as when we were kids?"

A shrug lifted Keri's shoulders. "It just reminded me of that time in sixth grade when Tammy Albright lied to Mr. Larken so he'd take the role of Juliet away from me and give it to her. Remember? She told him I said he had to give me the part because my dad was on the school board and could have him fired? The weasel gave her the part just to prove a point."

His eyes clouded for a minute as though he were trying to revive the memory, then a sudden grin split his face, sending Keri's heart into a tizzy. "That's right!" he said. "You showed up and sat with me on the front row. I remember how proud I was of you." He winked. "And if I remember right, that was the first time I held your hand."

"Could have been," she mumbled.

She remembered every warm, finger-laced second of it as though it had just happened yesterday.

"Anyway, remember how vindicated you felt when Tammy forgot half her lines?" He laughed. "Later, you flat-out told her God made it happen to teach her a lesson."

Resentment pinched her heart as the sweet hand-holding memory gave way to the humiliating aftermath. "Yes, and you embarrassed me by telling her that wasn't true. That one thing had nothing to do with the other."

"Well, what you told her *wasn't* true. You know God isn't going to make something bad happen to a twelve-year-old girl just because she took away the chance for Hollywood fame and fortune from you. Besides, didn't she still apologize and tell you she felt too guilty for lying and that was why she couldn't remember her lines?"

"Too little too late," Keri muttered.

"I can't believe it." His expression changed from amused to bewildered.

"Can't believe what?"

"You're actually holding a grudge against Tammy after all these years?"

If only she could deny it, but seeing the whole thing through his eyes brought it to its proper perspective. She gave him a lopsided smile. "Dumb, huh?"

His returning smile was dazzling and Keri hoped for her sake that he was still afraid of being walloped again. Because if he moved in, she doubted very seriously she'd have the strength to resist his arms or his kiss. As if reading her thoughts, his expression grew serious and his foot dropped to the floor. His arms unfolded and he stepped forward. "Keri…"

A scream shot like an arrow from the bedroom, piercing the air with terror. Justin spun around and pushed through the door with Keri on his heels. Josh sat huddled against the headboard, his eyes wide, face drained of color.

"Josh, honey, what happened?" Justin asked, sitting on the bed.

"He was here, I saw him outside the window trying to get in."

A lump formed in Keri's throat. Her pulse quickened and all of her senses alerted to danger. "Saw who, Josh?" she asked.

The little boy gave Justin a pitiful look and flung himself into his father's arms.

"Shh, son," Justin said, rubbing Josh's back and holding him close. "It's all right. No one is here. It was just a bad dream."

"Look," Keri said softly. "The curtain is all the way closed, honey. You couldn't have seen anyone."

"I saw him," Josh insisted.

"Who?" Justin held him out at arms' length and looked him in the eye. "Who do you think you saw?"

Josh gulped several breaths of air and seemed unable to form the words. Finally, he found his voice enough to whisper, "The man who killed Mommy."

Chapter Six

❧

"Justin, there's just no way anyone was out here." Crouched outside the window, Keri shook her head and pointed to the frozen earth. "The ground is covered with ice and snow. Even a bird or small animal would leave some sort of print." She stood up and faced him. "Look. No tracks. If there was anyone out here, he wasn't walking."

"He was dreaming?"

She nodded. "Almost certainly. And it's no wonder. He still hasn't adjusted to his mom's death."

There wasn't even a hint of condemnation in her assessment of the situation, so Justin didn't bother to insist upon his innocence. Instead, he studied her face, searched her eyes. He had to know if she was only trying to reassure him, or if she truly believed they were in no danger. "Are you sure about this?"

"Absolutely. Besides, how would Josh know what his mother's killer looks like?"

In the confusion, Justin hadn't considered that.

"Good point." He nodded. "Now I just have to figure out how to convince him it was just a dream."

"You can handle it." Keri patted his arm as she walked past him and headed for the wood pile next to the back door.

Justin fell into step beside her. "That's it? No advice?"

A shrug lifted her shoulders. She grabbed an armload of logs from the pile. "Open the door, will you?" she grunted under the weight of the logs.

"Good grief, Keri, give me the wood." Without waiting for her permission, he relieved her of the load. "Are you going to answer my question?"

"I've been trying to think of something, but I'm just not qualified to offer you any advice on that one. I'm not a counselor or a parent." She stopped and regarded him, earnest concern clouding her beautiful green eyes. "You're a good father. Anyone can see that. Just do what comes naturally and be as honest as you can without belittling his fear."

She hesitated as though she wanted to say something else, then thought better of it and turned to open the door.

"Wait. What else did you want to say?"

A frown creased her brow as she struggled to decide whether or not to go ahead.

"Come on," Justin prodded. "Spill it."

"All right, but you might not like what I have to say."

The corners of his lips turned up. "I often don't."

Her face hardened. "If you're not going to take me seriously, there's no point."

All amusement fled, and Justin nodded. "I'm sorry."

"Josh is obviously dealing with some deep hurt

about his mother's death. We just witnessed a vivid nightmare. But are you sure he didn't see something the night his mother was murdered?"

Justin gave a vehement shake of his head. "The police questioned the boys. They were both asleep upstairs at the time—thank God."

"It must be something else then. Do they know the police suspect you?"

"Not that I'm aware of."

"What happens when they find out? Especially if you go to prison?"

Keri's words slammed into Justin like a line drive to the gut. He couldn't bear the thought of what the boys would think of him. Would they believe he was capable of doing such a thing? Would they feel betrayed?

He collected a deep breath and returned Keri's gaze. "I know. I haven't thought of much else. Josh used to be even more outgoing and fun-loving than Billy, if you can imagine that." He shook his head. "It's as if when Amelia died, part of him died, too. And I don't understand it because they weren't that close."

"They weren't that close?" Keri's brow creased. "What child isn't close to his mother?"

Justin gave a short laugh. "The child who has the kind of mother my sons had. Let's just say she wasn't the maternal sort."

He knew he'd said too much when her eyes narrowed with suspicion. "You didn't love her?"

The question rankled him. Here he was trying to share his worries about his sons and she had to revert to cop-dom on him. "Don't start interrogating me, Keri. I know what it looks like, but to tell you the truth, no,

I didn't love her as a wife. We slept in separate rooms after the twins were born."

Compassion darted to her eyes, then fled as quickly as it had come. Her face became a stone mask, dashing Justin's hopes. "Look, Justin. I don't care what kind of relationship you had with your wife. It's a shame your boys didn't have the benefit of strong mother-love, but that doesn't change the facts. I don't want to know the intimate—or lack thereof—details of your life with another woman."

Her chin trembled. And that small involuntary action shot into Justin's heart and pierced his conscience. She was fighting her emotions enough without him adding to it. Part of him wanted to explore her vulnerability. To toss the wood aside and gather her close. To see if she would pull away this time or allow his kiss. But he couldn't do that to her. Not while she clearly wrestled with whether she should believe him or not. He smiled. "I'm sorry. You're right. I shouldn't involve you in this any more than you already are."

She reached for the doorknob, then stopped once more. "Justin," she said without turning around to face him. "I hope they find out that you are innocent. I don't want to believe you capable of this crime."

He stared after her as she disappeared through the door, wishing she could just believe in him without the proof. But he supposed that was too much to ask. Despair gnawed his gut. He couldn't blame her for not wanting to revive their relationship. He'd murdered their friendship with fifteen years of no contact.

He clenched his fist, pressing it tightly against his thigh to keep from putting a hole in the wall. He'd been through the house at least ten times in the past four hours, and there was nothing... Nothing! He'd scanned through every videotape in the video library——to no avail.

Where? Where could it be? Amelia had shown him the copy. But he'd taken that when he'd left her on the floor that night. She could have been lying about the existence of another tape, but he was sure she was on the level. Another copy of the tape existed, and he had to find it.

Keri turned another page, barely remembering what she'd just read. The entire afternoon had been filled with pages and pages of unintelligible words. With a frustrated huff, she tossed the book aside, rolled onto her stomach and buried her face in a fluffy pillow.

She hated feeling so conflicted. One second she was sure Justin was guilty—or reasonably sure—and then he'd do something like pray with his son, or smile so earnestly at her that she couldn't help but believe everything he told her.

The one thing she had known for sure over the last few years, the one thing, was that working for justice made her feel good about herself. It made her feel confident. Now in one day, Justin had ridden into town, and suddenly she was having second thoughts about doing her duty. Ten years of hard work down the tubes. The chance for the only decent cop position in Briarwood...down the tubes. All her brave words about being married to her job and not interested in marriage and children...down the tubes. She shuddered. Where had that one come from?

Justin had almost kissed her twice now. And the second time she'd practically begged for it. If Josh hadn't screamed bloody murder at the right moment, she'd be lost right now. Unable to take Justin into the jail. If he'd asked her, she'd have given in to her heart and run away like a fool. She'd be the worst kind of citizen: a corrupt cop, guilty of aiding and abetting a suspect—a fugitive from justice. Well, no. Not quite that. He wasn't under arrest yet. But if Raven's contact at the KCPD was correct, it could happen any second. Would she be able to push her feelings aside and still take him away from those boys?

In all likelihood, Justin was counting on just that thing. Why else would he be trying to kiss her so soon after becoming reacquainted? He'd obviously moved on without looking back when he left Briarwood. Probably had had scads of girlfriends over the years. Why would he be attracted to her? Last time she'd looked, she was no prize. Not a troll by any means, but nothing for someone like Justin to fall over himself about.

She pulled herself up from her bed and stood in front of the full-length mirror on the inside of the door. Red curls exploded from her head, giving her a wild appearance—not like the women in her romance novels, whose messy, curly locks always made the hero long to plunge his fingers through the mass.

Ha! Justin wouldn't be able to get his fingers through her hair without getting them stuck in her tangled, coarse mop. With a sigh, she grabbed her brush and a fat brown scrunchie from her dresser. Tugging and wincing, she brushed out the tangles and pulled back the riotous mass. She should chop it off, she thought with a sniff, as curls around her temples popped out of the band. It would make a lot more sense in her line of work. Only Dad's insistence that she was the "spitting image of her mother," kept her from it. Mom's hair was one of Dad's fondest memories. And if Keri admitted it, she liked the idea of resembling her mother so strongly. It comforted her to look in the mirror, see the resemblance and remember.

A knock on the door startled her. She jumped and pressed her hand to her racing heart. "What?" she barked.

"Well, aren't you a ball of sunshine?" Dad's voice drifted through closed door. "You have a phone call."

Keri twisted the doorknob and gave it a firm yank, coming face to face with Dad. "Who is it?" she whispered, taking the cell phone and covering the mouthpiece. "It's not the chief, is it? He told me not to try to go to town."

"It's Denni."

Hesitating, Keri frowned. What would her sister be calling out here for? Especially on a Tuesday afternoon? "If she called to cancel for Thursday, I'll kill her!"

Dad returned her frown. "Just talk to her. She don't have all day." He turned and headed back down the hall.

"Denni?" Keri closed the door and stretched back out on the bed, crossing her legs out in front of her.

"Hi!"

"You're not backing out on Thanksgiving are you? Dad really wants this."

"Not unless the weather stays bad. The main roads should be clear, though."

"So you're just calling to talk?"

"Actually, I called to ask if I can bring one of the girls. Everyone else has plans for Thanksgiving."

"Oh, sure. The more the merrier, you know that."

Denni had worked for years as a social worker. A few years ago, she'd grown disillusioned at seeing how many children grew up to become either welfare recipients or inmates in state prisons. She had opened a home for eighteen-year-old women just out of foster care. Finding work with her help, or filling out financial-aid packets for college was a prerequisite for living in her grand Victorian. Keri admired her more than anyone she knew.

"So, Dad tells me you have company up there in the Big Woods." She hedged a bit, obviously curious, but probably not wanting to press. As a social worker, Denni understood privacy, unlike their sister Raven, whose job as a reporter kept Keri on the defensive most of the time.

"Did Dad tell you who the company is?"

"Yeah…"

Releasing a heavy sigh, Keri adjusted her weight to her side and rested her head on her free hand.

"So what does he look like after all these years?"

A grin lifted Keri's lips. Always the romantic, of course Denni would want the essential information.

"Tom Cruise meets Brendan Fraser. Only better."

"Oh, wow."

"Yeah."

"So which one's mouth is his like?"

Warmth crept up Keri's neck, and she knew her face was red. "I guess it's more like Brendan's."

"Has he kissed you yet?"

"Denni! He's a suspect in a murder case!"

"Oh, come on, I find it hard to believe Justin is capable of murder. Besides, suspects can't kiss?"

Keri rolled her eyes and fought the urge not to divulge the information about the couple of close calls. Besides, the more she thought about those moments, the more humiliated she became and the more convinced that Justin was playing her. Cons tried it all the time with female corrections officers and cops. A good-looking prisoner could play on the vanity or poor self-image of a vulnerable officer. It had happened time and again. But she wouldn't let Justin do that to her. No way! She was not vulnerable to him.

"I can't get romantically involved with him."

"So that still doesn't answer my question. Come on…kiss or no kiss?"

"No! The guy is most likely going to the pen for a really long time, if not forever. I don't exactly think we should be discussing him like a potential prom date."

Keri could sense Denni sober. "You're right. Dad said he's got a couple of kids?"

Thankful for the change of subject, Keri stated, "Yeah, Billy's a real sweetie. He lights up the house." Her mind went back to the incident over the board game in the kitchen. "Josh is…let's just say he's been through a lot."

"Children deal with trauma differently."

"I guess. I don't know. It just seems like there's more to it. Like he's been touched in a way that Billy hasn't. I think he's dealing with a trauma Billy didn't go through."

"Like what?"

"I wish I knew."

"Does Justin have the boys in counseling? Or did he, before he took off?"

Ashamed, she hated to admit the truth. "I don't know. I never asked him. Never even occurred to me."

"Well, it's my job to ask that stuff. Don't worry

about it. There's nothing to be done right now, anyway. There may be counseling available for them once they enter the foster-care system. If it comes to that."

Keri tried to imagine Billy and Josh living happily in a foster home, but she had trouble conjuring up a convincing image. A sudden thought occurred to her and she sat straight up with a gasp. "Hey, they wouldn't split them up, would they?"

"They'd try not to. But you never know what homes are available."

"I hate this." She rested her forehead in the palm of her free hand. "I hate that those boys would have to be without their dad. Justin's a great dad. Even if they get to stick together, they'll be miserable without him."

"So you don't think he did it?"

"Did what?"

"Killed his wife?"

"Oh, I don't know. I hope not. I just said he's a good dad."

"A good father wouldn't kill his children's mother, Keri."

"That's not for me to decide. It's not for anyone to decide except a jury of twelve."

An exasperated sigh hissed through the line. "This is Justin Kramer we're talking about. I don't believe you can be as objective as you're trying to sound. It has to be eating you alive. You need to take a position and stick to it."

Keri's ire rose at the firmness in Denni's voice. When was her older sister going to stop bossing her around? "I don't have a position one way or another. I only mentioned on an impersonal level that I've noticed Justin takes adequate care of his boys. That doesn't mean I plan on letting him slip through my fingers again." Keri cringed. Had she really said *again?*

Denni's chuckled answered her question. "I knew you weren't over him."

"I didn't mean 'again.' I mean I'm not letting him go until I know for sure if he's going to be arrested. As in he's not getting away from me. 'Stop! Police!' And all that. So don't try to make me sound like a simpering, wishy-washy female cop."

"Oh, hey, speaking of that. Dad said you're up for chief. How great would that be if you got it? I can't even imagine a woman as chief of police there. That's like having a female president. Only bigger considering we're talking about Briarwood. Monumental."

Keri's mind raced, trying to keep up with Denni's line of reasoning. "Yeah, well, if I'm arrested for contributing after the fact, I'll pretty much lose all hope of that."

"So I guess you have to decide what's most important to you. Your job or helping an innocent man?"

"If he's innocent."

"He is. You know it in your heart."

Denni's words played over and over in Keri's mind long after they'd said goodbye. If she could only be sure Justin was innocent or guilty. At this point, she couldn't risk everything on a whim and a few tingles whenever he came close. When the phone rang again, she jumped. "Hello?"

"Keri, honey? This is Ruth. I'm seeing a car off the road here."

"Well, Ruth, you'll have to call the station. Remember I'm on vacation at the cabin with Dad?"

"Well, of course I remember! I'm not in town. I left the café in Doris's hands and hightailed it right out here."

"Ruth! What do you mean? Chief Manning said the crews weren't getting through."

"Oh, well, it was slow-going. Took me the better part of four hours to get here."

Four hours? The woman must have driven fifteen miles per hour the entire way.

"What are you doing here two days early?"

"When your Daddy told me about those sweet boys and your handsome Justin, I couldn't stay away. I figured you'd need more groceries, for one thing, and I picked up a few coloring books and some toys to keep the kids occupied."

The woman actually giggled. "Well, there's my cuddly bear standing on the front porch waiting for me. Yoo-hoo! Hi, honey cakes!" She clicked off the phone without saying goodbye.

Keri rolled her eyes and pressed the button to shut off the phone. It was downright embarrassing how much in love those two were. But, she had to admit, she loved Ruth and was glad her dad had found a woman he could dote on. She grinned and went to greet the object of her dad's affection.

Justin couldn't hide his surprise at Keri's suggestion they pull his car out of the ditch.

"What?" she asked, staring petulantly at him as though she were Oscar the Grouch caught in a random act of kindness.

He shrugged, unwilling to antagonize her and risk a change of heart. "Nothing. I'm ready whenever you are."

Scowling, she grabbed her coat, hat and gloves. "Well, don't read anything into it. Ruth suggested it. I just agree that we should get your car out of the ditch."

"All right." He slipped into his own coat and gloves and followed her outside.

She remained silent as she fired up the Jeep and waited for it to warm up. Only when she'd eased the vehicle onto the road, did she speak. "Got your keys?"

"Yep. Right here in my pocket."

She gave a practically imperceptible nod.

Justin cleared his throat. "So, Ruth is quite a pistol, isn't she?"

Keri's lips turned slightly up at the corners. "I think that's why Dad likes her. He likes unconventional women."

"I remember your mom being sort of a free spirit, too, wasn't she? I used to love coming over and tasting her new recipes or seeing new curtains."

Keri laughed. "She moved the furniture around every other week. She always needed something new." Her eyes clouded. "That's why she was out that night."

"The night she was killed?"

"Yes." Her voice came out a hoarse whisper. "She was painting the living room and ran out of paint. She had to drive thirty miles to Springfield to find a place still open at ten o'clock. She never made it to the store. The man who killed her had been drinking since four that afternoon. He was so plastered he doesn't remember the accident." Her voice choked and she drew a short breath. "He spent five years in prison. I heard that he returned to his happy home, and his wife and children welcomed him with open arms."

"Is this why you decided to become a cop?" Justin asked quietly. "Because of your mom?"

She shrugged. "I guess so. I had high hopes of closing down the bar in Briarwood. But of course that didn't happen. So I thought I'd intimidate the drunks to stay off the road. But just the other day, Junior Conner—" she glanced sideways "—remember him?"

"Vaguely."

"Anyway, just the other day, he got behind the wheel of his truck and almost killed a group of teenagers. I tell you, if I had my way, he'd go to prison for the rest of his life."

"Maybe he'll get some help while he's locked up," Justin replied.

"I'm sure he will. And he'll be sober for about thirty minutes after he gets out of jail."

Justin decided not to press. Better to stay on neutral ground for now. Keri was in no mood to consider the possibility of genuine rehabilitation.

Slowing the Jeep, she carefully maneuvered around so that they were headed back toward the cabin. "We'll hook up the chain. Even with four-wheel drive and chains on the tires, I don't know if we can get enough traction to get your car out of the ditch."

"It's going to be tricky. Want me to drive the Jeep?"

Her withering look was loud and clear. He grinned and held up his hands in surrender. "Sorry."

It took only a few minutes to connect the two vehicles with a heavy chain. While the engine warmed, he opened the glove box and pulled out his cell phone. He checked his messages. Four. All from Bob. All within the past three hours. The last one occurring only ten minutes before they got to the car.

Something must be up for him to call so many times in such rapid succession. Justin's stomach flopped. What if the killer had been found? Or what if the witnesses had admitted they were lying?

He punched in Bob's number. After several rings he got the answering machine.

He left a short message, pocketed the phone, and concentrated on steering while Keri pulled his car from the ditch.

Chapter Seven

So much for a peaceful two-week vacation, Keri groused to herself as she filled the sink with soapy water. It was bad enough that Justin's presence brought her nothing but anxiety, but now Ruth had breezed in with her exhausting, larger-than-life personality and upped the energy level in the small cabin about ten notches. She'd also brought a TV/VCR combo so the boys could watch cartoon videos. Not that Keri begrudged the boys a few minutes of fun, but what about *her* vacation? And being as how she and Ruth were the only single women occupying the cramped cabin, Keri had to share her room with the woman. And her bed.

With a half growl, she plunged her hands deep into the bubbles to locate the sponge. She attacked the dishes with vengeance, taking out her frustration on the remains of Ruth's special Texas-style fried chicken, mashed potatoes and gravy and green beans swimming in bacon grease. Had the woman never heard of light meals or reduced fat? Keri shook her head. How Ruth kept a pretty decent figure for a woman her age, she'd never guess.

As the pile of dishes began to shrink, Keri's mind bobbed from one person to the next until settling on Josh and Billy. She had to come up with some way to help them deal with their mom's death—especially Josh. He had barely said three words most of the day. Keri wasn't sure if it was because of the trauma of his horrible dream, or if he felt silly after Justin told him there was no evidence anyone had been outside of his window in the recent past. Regardless, everyone's attempts to draw the boy out of his shell today had failed. He'd barely eaten and had meekly surrendered to the bath Justin was currently overseeing.

The hollowness of Josh's eyes haunted Keri's memory until finally she couldn't bear it anymore. She left the dishes and sank onto a kitchen chair. Dropping her head into her hands, she gave in to her tears. Despair clenched her stomach, gripping it like a vise as the tears trickled down her face. Then, knowing tears alone wouldn't help the child, she began to pray. Deep, heart-wrenching entreaties rose from the center of her being on behalf of the boys Justin had brought into her life. Boys she wanted to wrap up in her arms and protect from the ugliness of what was surely to come to them in only a couple of days.

Then she prayed for Justin. He was trying desperately to be cheerful for the boys' sakes, but the sparkle she remembered so well in those blue eyes was glaringly absent. As though he'd lost his energy.

She looked up as the door swung open and, as though summoned by her thoughts, Justin appeared, the damp sleeves of his blue-denim overshirt rolled up to his elbows. A dark blue T-shirt stretched across a well-muscled chest. He dominated the room just by making an appearance. When he caught her eye, his lips turned upward. He dazzled her with his smile. A smile meant only for her. The kind of smile that girls like her waited for forever, but were rarely lucky enough to receive. Always a bridesmaid, never a bride. Always dreaming of Prince Charming, always disappointed.

"Are you okay? Why are you crying?"

Reality bit hard as the prince stepped fully inside and closed the kitchen door.

Keri sighed and stood, disgusted with herself for even thinking along those lines. By now, she should be smart enough to realize that if by some fluke the prince did show up, as he'd promised a million years ago, he'd be suspected of murdering his wife. So much for dreams. She scowled at him and headed back to the sink.

The sound of Justin's footsteps following her on the hardwood floor sent her heart racing. He stood beside her at the sink, but made no move to touch her. "I asked you a question. Are you okay?"

"Yeah." She sniffed. "Why?"

"Because your face is red and splotchy and your nose is starting to run. Here take this." He grabbed a tissue from the box on the counter.

Miffed by his unchivalrous mention of her red face and runny nose, she snatched the tissue and did what she had to do. When she felt sufficiently presentable, she tossed it away and went to work on the greasy iron skillet. "So you got the boys all bathed?"

"Yep. Bathed and settled into bed."

He snatched up a dishtowel and made himself useful drying the dishes already in the drainer. "Now, do you want to tell me why you're crying?" He leaned in closer to her and cocked his head. "It's not about me, is it?"

She sliced a look his way, then laughed at his teasing grin. "You're so conceited," she said, pushing him sideways with her shoulder.

"Seriously, though. Want to talk about it?"

She shrugged. "Not really."

"All right." He grabbed another plate.

"Well, if you really want to know, I was praying for Josh and Billy. The whole situation just makes me cry for them."

He stopped drying a glass container and put it down, then pressed her shoulder to draw her around. "Thank you, Keri." His eyes were misty, making them appear as clear as two lakes on a summer day. "You have no idea what it means to me to know someone besides me is praying for them." His voice broke. "Only God will get them through it. How much are they going to have to stand at such an age?"

Somehow, against all reasonable thought, she gathered him into her arms. He clung to her, his fingers pressing against her back as he drew her close and rested his head on her shoulder, taking her back to the day of his parents' funeral.

Keri hesitated only a moment, then slowly and methodically began to stroke his black hair, marveling at its softness. "It'll work out. I know it will. If you're innocent, like you say you are, then God will go to work on your behalf."

He pulled back. A frown pinched his brow. "*If* I'm innocent? What am I going to have to do to prove to you that I'm not capable of such an act?"

"I don't know, Justin. I want to trust you. You've no idea how badly. Do you think I want to believe that the boy I've loved all my life—" Her eyes widened at her admission and she hurried to amend her statement before he could pounce on it. "I mean, I don't want to believe the boy that I loved as a child, could be capable of murder." She moved away quickly, slapping away nonexistent dust from her thighs as she struggled to gain her composure. "I didn't mean that I love you anymore."

Justin leaned back against the sink while Keri attacked the chicken fryer with renewed energy.

"Sure, I know," he replied. But he didn't sound very convinced.

She squared her shoulders. "Anyway, I have to do my duty. If I just take your word, without proof, I could never bring myself to arrest you. Don't you see?"

Drawing a shaky breath, Justin nodded. "I know." He grabbed up his towel once more and they worked in silence for several minutes.

Too many emotions thickened the air, stifling Keri until she wanted to scream and rush outside into the cold air just for a five-minute reprieve. Instead, she drew upon the lightness of a few minutes before.

"You're pretty good at KP duty." Keri's words sounded flat despite her pitiful attempt to lighten the mood between them.

"I have lots of experience. KP is one of my main jobs at the mission."

The comment took her by surprise, and she glanced at Justin, genuinely interested. "What do you mean? I thought you did counseling."

"That's part of it. But there are also necessary chores to be done and not nearly enough volunteer workers. We feed about five hundred people every day along with the men who bunk there for however long they stay. That's only supper. If I had my way, we'd provide at least two meals daily, but the funds aren't there for now. Maybe eventually..."

Taken aback, Keri shook her head. "That's amazing. I'd love to be involved in something like that." The church benevolence program provided groceries for needy families in Briarwood, and though she'd donated funds for the program, Keri had to admit to little to no hands-on work.

"Really?" Justin's brow rose ever so slightly.

Keri's heart picked up at the intensity of his gaze, but her face grew hot at the surprised tone of his voice.

She rinsed the pan and set it in the drainer. "Well, yeah. Is that so hard to believe? That I'd want to help someone?"

Justin picked up the pan and rubbed the towel over it, keeping his gaze on hers. "No. I remember when we were kids we discussed being missionaries—"

"I don't want to discuss our childhood. Remember?"

He shrugged. "Where does this go?" he asked, holding up the dried-off skillet.

Keri took it from him and walked to the stove. "We'll be using it a lot so Dad just said leave it on top." When she turned back around, Justin still stood by the sink, but now he faced her, his arms folded across his chest.

"Regardless of whether you want to discuss our former relationship, what I meant was that I assumed since you didn't go into some sort of job where you were helping people, that you had given up on your desire for missions."

His comment raised Keri's hackles more than a little bit. "You don't think I'm helping people?"

"I'm not saying there's anything wrong with what you do. So don't waste your breath defending the worthiness of being a police officer. I know it's an important job. But cops wage a different kind of war on evil than the one I wage every day in the inner city. And personally, I believe you'd be happier if you'd stuck to the original plan."

With a shrug, she dismissed him and stomped to a kitchen chair. "Whatever." She sat, grabbing a magazine from a stack in the middle of the table, deciding to ignore him.

Justin grabbed a mug from the cabinet and poured a cup of freshly brewed coffee. "Want a cup?"

Shaking her head, Keri flipped a page.

Something akin to a growl escaped his throat as he took the chair across from her. "Oh, I see."

"See what?" Keri kept her eyes focused on the fascinating advertisement for the latest, most absorbent paper towels on the pages in front of her.

"You don't like what I have to say, so I get the silent treatment. Typical."

Keri slapped down the magazine and glared at him. "Typical? That's a bit chauvinistic, don't you think?"

The corner of his lip turned up in a sardonic half grin. The gloves were off. He was obviously making no attempt to win any points with her now. "I didn't mean typical of women." He raised his coffee cup to his lips. "I meant typical of you."

Leaning forward, Keri shot him what she hoped was her meanest look. "What do you mean, typical of me? You don't even know me, Justin Kramer. I am a grown woman, fifteen years more mature than the idiot who hung on your every word."

There that should do it. Effectively remind him that she didn't need him, didn't care what he thought of her and wouldn't have liked him when they were kids if she'd had any sense.

So why didn't he look like a guy who'd just been reduced to his proper place in this scenario? She frowned as he leaned in closer, his lips curved in a knowing smile.

"I don't know, Keri. I'm remembering exactly the way you were back then. A cute little redhead with enormous green eyes that dazzled me from the first time I can remember you—which is probably around five years old. From where I'm sitting, you haven't changed much…and neither have those eyes."

Keri sucked in a breath. If he was going to go there, she'd be putty in his hands. Two minutes. Tops.

"Justin…" she groused, warning thick in her voice.

"Want to know what else I'm remembering?" he asked.

"No."

"Too bad." He grinned. "I remember a girl who had to have everything just so. And if she didn't get her way, she pouted. And guess who always got the silent treatment? A lot like right now."

Okay, so maybe he did remember. But it wasn't like he ever put up with it, so what was he griping about?

"Oh, don't act like you were the martyr of our relationship!" Keri gave up all pretense of not caring. "I might have given you the silent treatment, but you were always the holdout and I always gave in. And you know it!" She cringed at the childish expression.

"Well," he said, leaning back in his chair until the front legs came off the floor. Once more, he folded his arms across his chest and gave her a lopsided smirk. "I was always right. Some things don't change, do they?"

Before she could consider her actions, Keri kicked out her foot and snagged his suspended chair leg. The motion took him by surprise and he tipped back, eyes wide, mouth open. He landed with a crash on the floor.

"Hey!"

Keri gasped in unison with his shocked response. They stared at each other, neither believing she'd actually done it.

"Justin!" she said, shooting to her feet. "I'm so sorry." Then the sight of his precarious position on the floor, still seated in the upended chair, struck her as funny and she started to giggle.

Justin's eyes narrowed. "You don't seem sorry."

"I know. I'm sorry," she said again, but the glare in his eyes only made her laugh harder. She extended her hand. "Here, I'll help you up."

"Thanks." He grabbed her hand, and she caught the glint in his eye, just as he pulled her to the floor beside him.

The door opened at that moment and Mac and Ruth stared at them, the same look of bewilderment in both faces. "What in the world are you two up to?" Mac asked.

Keri and Justin exchanged a glance and lost control. Laughter rumbled from Justin and rippled from Keri.

Dad shook his head and glared at Ruth. "Just like when they were kids," he mused. "In their own little world."

The words sobered Keri immediately, but Justin let out one more short laugh. "Told ya," he said with a triumphant grin. "You haven't changed as much as you might think. And neither have I."

He hopped to his feet, grabbed hold of her hands without asking, and pulled her to her feet. "Sorry, Mac. I fell over in the chair and Keri tried to help me up."

"Never mind," Dad said. "I don't even want to know how she ended up on the floor."

A cell phone chirped as Keri bent to pick up the chair.

"Dad! I thought you were going to turn that thing off. Are you afraid of a little peace and quiet?"

"For your information, that wasn't my phone, little girl." He scowled. "And maybe you want to keep a civil tongue in your mouth, huh?"

"Sorry," Keri muttered.

"Uh, that's mine, actually," Justin said, pulling a phone from his belt under his blue overshirt. He glanced at it, then at Keri, a question written in his eyes. "It's Bob, my lawyer."

"Forget it. We made our deal. One phone call per fugitive."

"Stop it, Keri," Dad said. "Why do you have to be so sharp?"

"It's all right," Justin spoke up before Keri could defend herself. "She's right. The deal was one phone call."

"Well, she doesn't have to be so sharp about it." Dad sent her a pointed glance and turned and stomped from the kitchen. Ruth, who had remained uncharacteristically silent throughout the ordeal, shrugged at her, brow raised to show she agreed with her hero, and followed him into the living room.

Sufficiently reprimanded, Keri expelled a breath, her cheeks puffing with the action. "Your lawyer, huh?"

Hope sprang into Justin's eyes. He nodded.

"Oh, all right. But only with the same rules as before. I'm not leaving the room."

His lips tensed into a grim line. He gave her a jerky nod, then softened his irritation with a wink.

Keri tried to harden her heart against him, but found herself drawn in. How was she supposed to guard herself when the Justin she remembered so well had shown up and once again captured her heart?

Justin dialed Bob's number, catching Keri's gaze.

Lifting her brow, she returned her attention to the magazine she'd been reading. Justin grinned inwardly. His teenage-boy feelings for her had returned with vengeance. If only they could return to those easy days before his parents had died.

Bob's machine picked up. Justin left a quick message then snapped the phone shut.

"He's not there?"

"He must be on the other line. He'll call back in a sec."

Keri nodded and glanced back at the magazine. Justin wondered if she was really concentrating on it, or simply avoiding a real conversation with him.

He studied her now as she sat with her knees propped against the edge of the table, magazine resting on her thighs. Subconsciously, she snagged a red curl and twisted it around her finger, and her lips twitched at something she'd read. Justin swallowed hard. What sort of future could they possibly have together? Even if he didn't go to jail? How could he put his complete trust in a woman who thought him capable of premeditated murder? Still, watching her now sent his pulse racing double-time.

"Justin, you're going to have to stop staring at me." She didn't look up.

"Who's staring?"

"You are, and you're making me nervous." She looked him in the eye. "So cut it out, okay?"

"I'm sorry," he mumbled.

"Oh, never mind." She shut the magazine and tossed it across the table. It landed atop the magazine pile, askew. "Do you want some more coffee?"

"Nah, it's too late."

Keri shrugged. "It's decaf. Dad has high blood pressure."

"Really? Didn't taste like it. Anyway, no thanks. Bob should be calling back in a sec."

The phone chirped just as Keri sat back down. She sent him a grin. Justin's heart turned over at the gesture, and he had a hard time trying to remember how to answer the phone.

He cleared his throat and pushed the on button. "Bob?"

"Yeah. I'm glad you're okay."

"Why wouldn't I be? Didn't Rick get in touch with you?"

"Yeah. I wish you had called me instead. I could have given Rick the message. We don't know who from the mission signed that affidavit. You have to be careful who you trust. My advice to you is to steer clear of anyone with ties to the mission for now. Even Rick, until we have more information."

His aggravated tone set Justin's own defenses on alert. "I needed to talk to him about the mission. You don't need to worry about Rick. Believe me. We've been friends for a long time. I trust him as much as I trust you."

"All right," Bob said abruptly. "Have it your way. I have to tell you something."

A chill trailed Justin's spine at the heavy sigh on the other end of the line. "What happened?"

"First of all, they won't tell me who the witnesses are since you're not officially arrested and arraigned. But that's not all I had to tell you." Bob hesitated a moment and cleared his throat.

Nothing like starting off with the good news. Justin cringed and braced himself.

"Your home was broken into."

"What? Was anything stolen?"

"Nothing that we can tell. Your electronics and computer are all still there. Clearly, whoever broke in was looking for something in particular."

"Did they find it?"

"We don't think so. It seems your housekeeper has been keeping a pretty close eye on the place since you've been gone. She told the police she saw the glow from the flashlight and pulled into your driveway. We think that scared him off."

Mrs. Angus was a pistol. He should have known she'd try to do some sleuthing on her own. Justin shook his head. "I should have let her know I was leaving. I hope someone told her to stay put and not try to play Miss Marple."

"The police scolded her, but I'm not sure it did any good."

"Probably not. So where does this leave things with the police? Does it throw suspicion off me?"

"Well, they *have* been concerned that you might have been kidnapped or killed. Since you obviously didn't let them know you left town."

"I'm sure they've been frantic with worry," Justin drawled.

"Their other theory is that you broke in yourself to cast suspicion elsewhere."

A groan rose and left Justin's throat. Keri glanced up, frowning. "Justin?"

He shook his head.

"Bob, do you think it was Amelia's killer? Or do you think the break-in was random? Was anything missing?"

"Since nothing of value was taken, it looks like whoever broke in was looking for something in particular. Do you have any idea what that might be?"

"I don't have a clue."

"What about…" Bob hedged.

"What about what?" Justin prompted.

"Do you think Amelia was involved in anything shady? Something that could have gotten her killed?"

"I don't really think there's any question of whether she was killed because of shady dealings. Why else?" Irritation made another untimely appearance, and Justin wanted to pound his fist on the table to take out the stress of his own helplessness.

"But specifically." Bob's voice held the same hint of frustration Justin felt. "If we could just narrow down the choices, it would give us something to go on. A lead. The first step in the right direction."

"I hear what you're saying, Bob. I just don't know what you're getting at. How would I know what she was involved in?" He scrubbed his jaw, and glanced upward at the ceiling as if the answers would be found in the wood planks. "Drugs, maybe?"

"The police surely would have found any kind of drugs."

"That's true."

"I was thinking…wondering really."

Bob's obvious hesitation to state what he was thinking sent warning bells through Justin. He wasn't sure he wanted to hear what his friend suspected.

"What were you thinking?" he asked to break the nerve-wracking silence over the lines.

"What about blackmail?"

A short laugh burst from Justin's lips. "Blackmail? Oh, come on. Amelia? Who could she have possibly been blackmailing?"

"That's what I hoped you could answer."

Bob's terse reply sobered Justin. "I'm sorry, Bob. I just can't picture Amelia in that role."

"Maybe that's always been your problem where she was concerned. You never thought she was capable of the things she did…until you caught her red-handed. Maybe this time she pushed the wrong guy too far. Not everyone is as forgiving as you are. Anyway, be thinking about it. Maybe now that you've been presented with the possibility, you'll remember something that might help you."

"I'll try, Bob." A sense of urgency engulfed him. "If Amelia was blackmailing someone, why would he kill her before he got what he wanted from her? Why kill her then have to wait months to go after what he was after?"

"I'm afraid I'm not clairvoyant. We'll have to wait and see. My best guess is that she made the killer so mad he snapped and put a bullet in her head before he realized he hadn't gotten what he came to get."

"You sound pretty certain."

"I've been around this scene for a long time, Justin. I know when there's more to a story than meets the eye. The two things I'm sure about in this whole mess are that Amelia got what she had coming, and that you didn't do it. All I want to do is prove it so we can both get on with our lives."

As he fell silent, Justin could feel his friend's anger hovering just below the surface. If they hadn't known each other for so long, Justin might have missed it altogether. But he could tell this was bothering Bob deeply.

"Bob, listen. I know you want to see me cleared. And I appreciate how deeply it's affecting you. But how about taking a little time off? Take your wife out for dinner and a movie."

"I doubt she'd want to go."

"I know things have been strained between you two. But I also know how much you love each other. Keep God at the center of your relationship and everything will work out between you."

A cynical laugh shot through the line. "You're the strongest Christian I know and things didn't work for you and Amelia."

"True." The knife twisted with that remark, but Justin knew his friend was speaking out of his own frustration. "But Amelia didn't know or want to know the Lord." He glanced up. Keri had given up all pretense of thumbing through another magazine.

Red splotches dotted her cheeks as his gaze locked on to hers. Emotion flickered in her green eyes, and Justin's heart soared. No matter how hotly she tried to deny it from now on, the jig was up. He knew she believed him. He reached forward and took her hand, lifted it, and pressed a kiss.

"Still there, Justin?"

"Yeah," he said, his voice hoarse as he moved his thumb over the back of Keri's hand. Nervously, she wet her lips, and he nearly dropped the phone. "Listen, Bob. I'm praying. But I have to go. Page me again if you get any more information."

"One more thing, Justin."

"What?" he asked impatiently. His eyes moved over Keri's face, resting on her lips. He wanted to end the conversation quickly and gather her into his arms. Though he wasn't sure exactly what could happen, he knew they'd turned a corner.

Obviously sensing the same thing, Keri drew a shaky breath. She pulled her hand away and stood. "You can say goodbye in private," she whispered. "I'm going to bed."

He wanted to call after her to wait, but Bob's voice brought him back to the present conversation. "Justin, I know you think you can trust your friends. But I'd be careful with Rick."

"Oh, come on."

"I know he's a minister and you two have been friends a long time, but just please be careful what you tell him."

"There's nothing to tell him at this point, anyway."

"What about your location. Does he know that?"

"No. Well, I told him I'm at a cabin with the boys."

"Good. Good. We'll keep it between you and me, then. I think you can go ahead and tell me now."

"We're at a cabin at Lake Bennett."

"Do you know how long you'll be gone?"

"Probably until Monday. Unless the police get their arrest warrant sooner. Then I'll come back and turn myself in."

After a couple minutes went by, Bob said goodbye. Justin stared at the door, regret filling him that Keri had taken off like a scared rabbit. But there was always tomorrow. He only prayed God would grant him another moment like the one he'd shared with Keri a little while ago. The image of having her in his arms almost overwhelmed him.

He stood and grabbed the cup she'd left on the table. As he reached the sink and turned on the water to rinse it out, a sudden thought slammed into him. How could he even think of declaring his feelings to a woman when he was very likely going to jail in a few days? Only a jerk would take advantage of this situation.

He set the mug in the drainer and dried his hands. Leaving the kitchen, he glanced into the living room and smiled at the sight of Ruth and Mac snuggled together on the couch watching an old movie together.

God willing, that will be Keri and me some day. He smiled at the thought, even as his eyes filled at the futility of such a dream.

Chapter Eight

A wide yawn stretched Keri's mouth as she pushed open the kitchen door. She set her Bible and devotional book on the table and padded over to the counter to make coffee. Sleep had eluded her all night except for a snatch here and there. Between sharing a bed with the undisputed champion of sleep kickboxing, and thinking about the phone conversation she'd overheard just before bed, she felt haggard and in desperate need of a pick-me-up.

She opened the cabinet over the coffeepot, wormed her hand through a maze of decaf coffee, tea—instant and brewable—sugar, flour and a variety of miscellaneous items that had most likely been there for years, and produced a small can of real coffee. The caffeinated variety.

Before Dad got up, she'd have it gone and a fresh pot of decaf brewed for him. Since a scare with his blood pressure five years earlier, Keri had been the caffeine and salt police. She'd even eased up on real coffee herself, except for an occasional latte, but this morning called for some heavy ammo.

Like a tiger stalking its prey she stood over the pot,

watching the French roast drip into the decanter with aching slowness. Her heavy lids lowered then opened again more than once while she waited. Finally, she grabbed a twelve-ounce mug from the cabinet and filled it, added the contents of two pink packets of artificial sweetener, and shook a mound of powdered creamer into the mix. She stirred and watched with satisfaction as the coffee lightened to almost white. Perfect.

She sipped while she walked to the table and took her seat. Her Bible and devotional book stared back at her from where she'd set them, and she reached forward. Would today's devotions bring life-changing revelation, or would the words be just that—empty words—black ink on white paper? Her heart as heavy as her eyes, she opened the devotional first.

Are you living your God-given destiny, or have you planned your own course?

Now fully awake, Keri almost gasped. She picked up the book and inspected it for any signs of dog-earing or any other tampering Justin might have done to prove his point from last night—that she wasn't doing what they'd felt called to do as children, and he had answered that so-called higher calling. On the verge of slamming the book shut, Keri stopped short as her eyes caught another phrase.

Emotional experiences during our growing-up years often dim our true purpose in life.

Like Mom's death leading me into law enforcement instead of my going into missions as Justin and I spent hours dreaming of when we were kids?

After taking only a second to ponder, she shoved the thought aside as ridiculous. Children often wanted to be firemen, teachers, famous singers, movie stars, all the occupations they admired most, but as adults they rarely became what they dreamed of. Right? Besides, even if she'd still wanted to be a missionary as she grew up, it wouldn't have been possible. With Mom gone and Denni and Raven away at college, Keri had had no choice but to stay in Briarwood and look after Dad. It wouldn't have been right for her to have pulled up stakes and gone halfway across the world when she had responsibilities at home.

Being a cop, following in Dad's footsteps, had been the best decision she could have made. She jutted her chin. No matter what Justin thought about it. No matter if her reasons hadn't been entirely motivated by her heart's hidden dreams. She had done what she'd needed to do and that was that. Besides, always in the back of her mind had been the thought that if she went away, Justin would come back to Briarwood and find her gone.

Squirming under her humiliating self-admission, she set the book aside and picked up her Bible instead. Turning to a familiar scripture, she allowed her heart to calm as she took comfort in the Proverb:

> Trust in the Lord with all your heart; do not depend on your own understanding. Seek his will in all you do, and he will direct your paths.

Suddenly the warm feeling she usually gained from the verse left, only to be replaced by the swift slice of a double-edged sword. What had once salved and quieted her soul now slashed at her conscience. Had she trusted the Lord with her life? Had she even bothered to seek His will? The path she'd been walking for the past ten years stretched behind her, rolling like a film. She recognized frustration, insecurity and discontent in her life movie.

Tears pricked her eyes. Had the last ten years of her life been nothing but futility? *Did I waste my life, Lord? And if so…can You give back my time and show me the divine plan You mapped out before I was conceived?*

She would have taken more time to delve into the prayer, but a loud banging on the back door nearly sent her through the roof. With a frown, she cautiously approached, pulled back the curtain, and yanked the door open in surprise. "Raven!"

Red-cheeked from the cold, her sister stomped the snow from her boots before she stepped over the threshold and grabbed Keri for a tight, quick hug.

"How come you didn't knock on the front door?" Keri asked.

"I saw Dad sleeping on the couch and didn't want to wake him. I figured you'd be in here drinking coffee. Early bird."

Keri grinned. "Yep. Want some?"

"Is it real?"

Keri nodded and walked to the cabinet to get a cup. "What are you doing here so early? We didn't expect you until tomorrow. How bad are the roads?"

Slipping out of her coat, hat and gloves, Raven answered the questions in reverse order. "The main roads aren't too bad—the driving lane is mostly clear on the four-lane. But this highway is a sheet of ice. I had to crawl to keep from ending up in a ditch. Lucky for me,

I was the only one on the road. Anyway, I had a few extra days and decided to spend them here. Besides, I wanted to get here ahead of the next system blowing in today." She gathered a deep breath. "And Dad told me about Justin and the boys."

Instinctively, Keri studied Raven's face to find traces of deception. "You're not here for a scoop, are you? Because I'm not going to let you use Justin to get a headline."

She poured the coffee, grabbed the sugar and powdered creamer with the other hand, and set all of it in front of her eldest sister.

"Like you could stop me if that's what I wanted to do," Raven baited.

The old rivalry popped up, and Keri's defenses went on red alert, then slackened to yellow when Raven smiled—semi-convincingly. "Dad told me Justin was set up. I'd like to help."

Narrowing her gaze, Keri kept her armor on. "What do you think you can do?"

Raven stirred the contents of her cup and took a sip. "I'm an investigative reporter. What do you think I can do? I'm going to get the facts of the case from Justin and see what I can dig up when I get back to Kansas City. By the way, Justin and the boys have been making the news, anyway. Giving his side of the story might help gain public sympathy."

Panic rose up and exploded from Keri's lips. "It would also give away his location! He came here to find a little peace and quiet before…" She couldn't bring herself to say "before he's arrested."

"Decide, Raven. Do you want to help or not? You can't be here as a reporter. Only a family member and friend."

"Calm down, little sister. I didn't really mean it. Let's work together to clear Justin's name. Maybe he'll give me an exclusive when it's all over."

Suddenly wishing she'd opted for decaf, Keri forced herself to relax.

"So what's he like after all these years?" Raven's smile hinted at teasing.

Refusing to bite at the insinuation, Keri shrugged. "He's a father trying to keep his life together for the sake of his sons."

Raven grinned even more broadly. "Denni said you were pretending you don't care. But we all know you do. You have that glow of a woman in love."

Slapping her hands on the table, Keri glared. "What I have is a stress blush because you breezed in and drove me crazy in ten minutes."

Tossing back her head, Raven let up a howl. "I knew it! You're a goner. Now we definitely have to prove Justin's innocent. How would we explain it to our friends if our cop sister was in love with an inmate at the DOC? That's just a little too talk-showy to be real."

Before Keri could formulate and deliver a crushing retort, the kitchen door swung open and Mac stumbled in. "What's all the racket in here?" Then his eyes lit upon Raven and his entire face brightened. "My baby's home! Why didn't you wake me up?"

Raven shot to her feet and flew into her dad's arms. A twinge of jealousy snaked through Keri as it always did when Dad showed Raven special affection. Keri had Mom's hair and features, but Raven took after her in all the ways that mattered. Her love of life, her tendency to throw caution to the wind and deal with the consequences later, her love of art and music; all those things were Raven, and Dad couldn't get enough of his eldest child, though he only saw her when Raven deigned to grace them with her presence once or twice a year.

"What are you doing, driving those roads, my girl?" he scolded, holding her at arm's length and devouring her with his gaze. "You could have been killed."

"No way," Raven said. "I'm too mean to die. You know that. Only the good die young." The words hung in the air, heavy and mournful, shrouding the joy of reunion and worst of all, dimming the light in Dad's eyes. Keri could have strangled her sister. "I'm sorry, Dad. I didn't mean that…"

Drawing Raven close, he pressed a kiss to her forehead. "Think nothing of it, darlin'. We can't weigh every word against a tragedy that occurred many years ago. You've said nothing wrong."

Keri blinked back her tears and cleared her throat. "Let me make a fresh pot of coffee, Dad."

"Sure, sure. You do that, honey." Just before she turned around to walk to the counter, Keri saw a frown on his face as he leaned in closer to Raven. "She makes me drink that fake stuff while she drinks the good coffee every time my back is turned."

"That's terrible," Raven said, sympathy thickening her voice. "Have mine. I only took a sip."

Spinning around, Keri snatched the mug up before Dad could reach for it. "Are you crazy?" she demanded, glaring at Raven. "Dad's on mega doses of blood-pressure meds. Do you want to kill him?"

Dad's eyes narrowed, but he didn't have a chance to tear into her as Raven's exasperated voice shot back.

"We were kidding around, Keri. Dad knows I'm not going to offer him something that's bad for his health. We were only teasing to get a rise out of you."

"Well, it worked. I hope you're both happy!" She tossed a dishtowel onto the table to clean up the mess she'd made by sloshing the coffee.

Get hold of yourself, Keri Mahoney. You're reverting to youngest-child syndrome, and Raven's eating it up. You're a mature woman with a career and you have nothing, absolutely nothing to feel inferior about!

"Josh!" Justin's panicked voice filtered through the house, breaking Keri out of her personal dilemma. "Josh! Where are you?"

Keri barreled through the kitchen door and nearly collided with Justin. He grabbed her arms to steady them both, his eyes wild with fright, his hair tousled from sleep.

"What's going on?" Her heart caught in her throat at his colorless face.

"Josh isn't in bed or the bathroom. I've looked everywhere. Is he in the kitchen?"

"No. He's not in there." A bubble of panic rose inside Keri.

Justin seemed to be frozen in place. Keri knew she'd have to snap out of it and take charge. "Go out front," she ordered, giving him a little shove back through the kitchen door. "I'll check in back."

Without waiting for permission, she grabbed Raven's discarded coat, hat and gloves and slipped them on as she exited the warm kitchen.

She stood on the porch and glanced into the gray dawn. There was no sign of the child. After a quick survey of the surrounding area, an idea shifted her focus from the freezing cold to a more likely explanation. She hurried in to the bedroom and headed for the closet. The closet light seeped from under the door. A smile of relief curved her lips.

"Josh, honey," she said softly. "It's just Keri, I'm going to open the door."

Twisting the knob, she pulled the door open. Her heart clenched within her chest at the sight of the little boy, his knees pulled to his chin, forehead resting on his knees. She crouched down in front of him and smoothed a hand over his unruly blond curls. "What are you doing in here, Josh?"

He shivered and looked up at her with mournful blue eyes. "I saw him again," he whispered.

Compassion washed over Keri. "It was only another nightmare, sweetheart. Come on. Let's get you back to bed to warm up those icy feet and hands. Your dad's worried sick about you." His body remained compliant as she lifted him and headed toward the bed.

"Miss Keri?" Josh whispered.

"Yes?" Keri laid him on the mattress and covered him with the quilt.

"Is it wrong if I know something really bad and I don't tell it?"

Careful not to show her keenness to be the recipient of his information, Keri shrugged. "I guess that depends on what that something is."

"Do they put kids in jail?" He looked up at her, trouble clouding his beautiful eyes. Trouble no child should have to deal with, as far as Keri was concerned. She crouched so that she met him eye to eye and placed her hands on either shoulder. "They don't put kids like you in jail, Josh. Is there something you feel you need to tell me? You don't have to be scared. I'm not going to let anyone hurt you."

"Josh! Thank God he's okay." Josh's eyes grew wide and he jumped away from Keri's touch as Justin made his appearance in the doorway and hurried across the room.

Keri recognized the look of apprehension that crossed the little boy's features even as he went willingly into his father's arms. Once again doubt crept in and threatened her fledgling faith in Justin. Had Josh been about to open up to her? If so, what was he going to say? That he'd witnessed his dad kill his mom? Dread nearly gagged Keri. She inched backward toward the door, then headed to the kitchen.

She stepped into the kitchen just as Dad was returning from outside. "You find him?" he asked.

Keri nodded. "In the closet."

Dad shook his head. "Poor tyke."

Raven let out a low whistle under her breath. "That was some drama."

"Yeah," Keri said noncommittally. Curiosity burned inside her. What had Josh been about to tell her when Justin showed up?

"Well?"

Keri turned to see her petite sister, her dark eyes sparkling with demand, her palms resting on slender hips. "Well, what?"

"Are you going to tell me what that was all about? What was the kid doing in the closet?"

"He had a nightmare."

"In the closet?"

Keri scowled. "No. It's a long story."

"Look, Keri. I know you think I'm just a nosy big sister out to steal away Dad's affection, but I really do want to help. If you fill me in on the details, maybe I can make some suggestions, phone calls, whatever. I'm not going to do anything to harm Justin or his boys. I give you my promise." Her dark eyes pleaded, and Keri felt herself caving. But she felt the need to get a couple of things straight before she let Raven in on the situation completely.

"First of all, I don't think you're out to steal Dad's affection. I think you break his heart every time you promise to come visit and then don't. That's the problem I have with your relationship with Dad. I'd welcome his happiness."

"All right. I take back my comment. I'm sorry, okay?"

"Second of all, I can't tell you anything until I get Justin's approval. This is his life and his son's nightmares we're talking about. So we'll see what he has to say about it later. After Josh settles down."

Raven gave a reluctant nod. Then she grinned. "So has Justin kissed you yet?"

Justin paced the room watching Josh lying flushed and feverish beneath a heavy quilt. He could only guess how long his son had huddled in that freezing-cold closet, shivering and terrified while he himself slept peacefully, dreaming of a future with Keri Mahoney.

Self-accusing thoughts accosted him over and over until Justin wanted to shout for his mind to shut up and give him five minutes of peace. What kind of parent was he? the silent voices demanded to know.

A gentle tap at the door pulled him from his brooding. "Come in," he called softly. His heart picked up at the sight of Keri standing in the doorway, her hair pulled back from her face. She was dressed in snug jeans and a loose, emerald green ribbed turtleneck that perfectly offset her fair skin and red hair. He motioned her into the room. With a half smile, she tiptoed across the wood floor.

"How is he?" she asked, standing over Josh's bed.

Her concern was so genuine, Justin took her hand. She didn't protest, but turned her palm flat to his, lacing their fingers. Justin took comfort in the simple gesture and didn't stop to examine its meaning. "He's still running a fever, but at least he's stopped shivering under the quilt."

"Good. Dad says it's most likely just a cold and probably has nothing to do with his adventure in the closet. He'll be okay in a day or so."

"I hope so."

Keri squeezed his hand. "He's a strong little boy."

Still holding her hand, Justin sat on the bed beside Josh. Keri stepped closer and brushed her free hand over his head. Pressing his forehead into her waist, Justin closed his eyes. He felt her lips brush against the top of his head.

"Why don't you let me sit with him for a while," she suggested. "Dad's watching a John Wayne movie with Billy. I'm sure they'd welcome your company."

Opening his eyes, Justin pulled back and studied her for a moment. She returned his gaze with steady appraisal. "You believe me now, don't you? Last night when I was talking to Bob I felt like…"

She slipped her hand from his. "Don't ask me to give you an answer to that question just yet, Justin. I'm not ready to say what you want to hear."

Disappointment twisted inside him. He stood. "I think I will go sit with Billy and your dad awhile."

"One word of caution."

Justin braced himself, not sure he was up for any more bad news. "Yeah?"

A grin tipped her lips. "Stay out of the kitchen. Raven and Ruth are clashing about what spices actually go into a pumpkin pie. It was starting to turn ugly in there when I snuck away."

Forcing himself to return her smile, Justin nodded. He appreciated her attempt at lightness after the events of the morning, but he couldn't quite convince his own heart to lift. A man could take just so much before things overwhelmed him. Justin was just about at that point. He swallowed back the sudden lump in his throat and cleared his throat. "Thanks again, Keri. Don't leave him alone even for a minute, okay? I don't want him to wake up from another nightmare and be afraid."

"I'll take care of him. Trust me."

If only you could take your own advice and trust me, he thought as he stepped into the hallway and carefully closed the door behind him.

Chapter Nine

With aching tenderness Keri sat in a straight-back chair next to the bed and watched Josh's angelic face as he slept. His wasn't even close to the sleep of the peaceful, a fact she acknowledged from his shifting, moaning and spastic eye movement. Her heart swelled with compassion, but even more with the startling newness of what could only be maternal love. *He should be my son, Lord. Mine and Justin's.* She drew in a deep, troubled breath. What's going to happen to him?

From the recesses of her imagination, Keri found an image of herself cooking and cleaning, playing in the yard, reading bedtime books, overseeing homework and doing loads of laundry. Her stomach knotted with the power of the desire for that image to become reality. She refused to allow Justin's beautiful image to spill over into the mini-film. She wasn't ready for that heartbreak just yet. Could she bear it if Josh told her he'd witnessed Justin kill Amelia?

A chill began at the base of her spine and crawled upward until it reached her shoulders and became a violent shudder. She stood and crossed silently to the window.

She pushed back the deep-blue curtain. Staring out at the gray world, she wondered what was in store for the unlikely group huddled together in the small cabin. Here they were, nestled in a secluded part of the world, an unlikely hodgepodge of human beings fitted together for different reasons. Topping the list were a grizzled ex-cop and his senior-citizen girlfriend, whose purpose was to bring the family together and gain some acceptance from Dad's three girls before they formally set a date for the wedding.

Then there was Raven, an investigative reporter, whose motives weren't entirely clear to Keri. Maybe she wanted to help. Maybe she wanted a scoop. One thing was clear, she wasn't happy about Dad's bride-to-be. Keri dreaded Raven deciding to voice her opinion. It would happen. Raven wasn't one to hold back for something as trifling as politeness. Most important, in the group were two precious look-alikes with very different concerns in the world.

Keri leaned her head against the cold glass. Oh, Justin. Justin—possibly a murderer, possibly the same wonderful soul mate she'd grown up loving with her whole heart. Guilty or not, all he wanted was to keep his family together for as long as he could.

And she capped off the unlikely group, a policewoman with a promotion on the line. As chief, she had a much better chance of influencing procedural changes in dealing with drunks like Junior Conner. Irritation bit at her. Who said just because Briarwood was a throwback to Mayberry that they had to treat the town drunk the same way Andy treated Otis? Junior had narrowly missed plowing into a bunch of kids during his latest binge. It was time to be a little more heavy-handed with him before he killed someone.

As chief, she would definitely make the town safer from the Junior Conners of the world, even if she had to stand outside the Drink 'n' Dance every Friday and Saturday night and watch as patrons left the bar. If she had to arrest every single person with an elevated blood alcohol content, she would——from the stay-at-home moms out for a night away from the kids, to the career drunks who were addicted to the hard stuff. Whatever it took to make sure that no more mothers in Briarwood were taken from this world when their daughters were on the brink of womanhood and needed them most.

On the bed, Josh moaned, mumbling, his words un-intelligible, his fear palpable even in sleep. Keri went to him and was about to reach out when he sat bolt up-right and screamed like a banshee.

"Josh, honey," Keri said, sitting next to him and try-ing to still his flailing arms. "It's all right. You're safe."

"I dreamed him again, Miss Keri."

The little boy buried his silken head in Keri's neck. She held his quivering body close, stroked his hair and began to pray. "Father, You've promised to give us peace while we sleep, even in the middle of a huge storm. You see that Josh is ill and dealing with a storm of fear and hurt right now. Please, give him peace and remind him that You are bigger than anything in the whole world. Let him know that I'm going to do what-ever it takes to keep him safe. In Jesus's Name, Amen."

During the course of the prayer, Josh had slowly re-laxed. Now he pulled away and settled back onto his pillow. Keri smiled at the look of peace that had replaced the fear in his eyes. *Thank you so much, God.*

Justin's eyes misted at the scene playing out before him. He'd charged down the hallway when Josh had screamed, but had stopped short when, on opening the door a crack, he saw Keri comforting his son effectively. His heart melted at the sight. The boys needed maternal love. He could give them food, clothing, shelter—all the things a father should provide. The one thing he was not capable of giving was maternal affection—the soft touch that God had reserved for women's hands. What would it be like for the boys to have a real mother? Someone who would place their needs over hers? Amelia had loved the boys in her own way, but she had just been too selfish to give that mothering touch. He'd tried to be both mother and father, but he knew he'd been woefully inadequate.

Josh had completely relaxed in Keri's gentle arms—faster than he calmed when Justin held him after a nightmare.

"Miss Keri?"

"Yes?"

"Remember what I asked you before?"

"Yes, I remember. Do you want to finish telling me what you know that's so bad you're afraid to tell anyone?"

Justin's heart picked up. Instinctively, he pressed closer. Could Josh possibly have seen something that would prove his innocence? Shame filled Justin at the hope rising inside him. Shame at eavesdropping and hope that his nine-year-old son had seen his mother's killer.

What was wrong with him? And why was he just sitting here waiting for a warrant to be issued? He had to do something to prove his innocence. For his sons. For Keri.

"Do you want to tell me now, Josh? It's just the two of us in here. No one else will hear."

Josh's muffled reply evaded Justin's hearing. He pressed closer, desperate to uncover the reason behind Josh's behavior—the constant nightmares and emotional roller coaster. He released a frustrated breath at his inability to hear anything.

A tug on his sleeve startled Justin, and he jerked his head over and looked downward to meet Billy's scowl. "Daddy, you're missing the movie!"

Justin cringed. Guilt shot through him; he'd just been caught eavesdropping and there was no escape. He released a heavy sigh and waited for the inevitable.

"Hang on just a sec, Josh." Keri's voice held an edge of irritation. In a second the door flew open and Justin met her accusing glare.

Today was a good day. Not all days were. Often she sat silently, staring across the room as though she hadn't heard a word he'd spoken. Frustration drove him from the house on those days. He felt responsible for their not having a child by now. He'd tried. Gone through all the testing available, had taken fertility drugs to increase their chances of conceiving. To no avail. His darling blamed him. Even when she didn't say it, he could see the accusation in her gorgeous violet eyes. Now those eyes looked fondly upon him, though she didn't speak.

His heart soared. Life was worth living as long as she loved him. That's why he'd had no choice but to get rid of Amelia. He couldn't let her tell his wife about the baby. She must never know that he'd been able to give Amelia something he couldn't give the woman he loved.

At first he'd laughed in Amelia's face, disbelieving. But she'd proven she was pregnant—shown him the doctor's records. And the one fact he knew was that Justin didn't have anything to do with it. She'd seduced him. Tempted him until he couldn't help himself. Laughed at him for feeling guilty. Had allowed herself to get pregnant and threatened to destroy everything that meant anything to him. Unless she got what she wanted.

Money for silence. That's all she'd wanted. A half grin lifted his lips at the irony. The woman was definitely silenced. She'd left him no choice. It was her own fault. If only she'd never approached him in the first place, she'd still be alive.

Now he needed to find that tape and there would be no way for anyone to prove Justin didn't kill Amelia.

His eyes devoured his wife's beautiful face again and leaning forward, he pressed his lips against an unresponsive mouth. He pulled back with a weary sigh. It had been so long.

But she'd love him again. One look at those boys and things would be as they had been.

"You're going to be a wonderful mother, darling."

Chapter Ten

Frustration burned a hole in Keri throughout the morning hours as she worked side by side with Raven preparing a feast for the next day's Thanksgiving dinner. Ruth had excused herself, begging the need for a nap. Keri figured, more than fatigue, the woman just couldn't stand Raven's obvious disapproval and Keri's sullen silence one more minute. Who could blame her?

Pulling a freshly baked pumpkin pie from the oven, Keri could take no pleasure in the wonderful aroma steaming from the dessert.

For the second time in one day, Josh had been about to tell her something important. At least Keri *felt* it was important and would be relevant to the case. Twice Justin had intervened. Coincidence? Maybe. Or maybe a little too much to be coincidence.

He'd made a point of staying with Josh after she'd caught him red-handed eavesdropping on her conversation with the boy. Now they were snuggled together on the couch, Josh wrapped up in a blanket and nestled on his father's lap. A sight that might have melted every defense in Keri's mind and heart if not for the niggling suspicion that Justin was purposely keeping her away from Josh.

Suppressing a growl, she dropped the pie onto a cooling rack on the counter.

"Hey, take it easy," Raven said, snatching the oven mitts from Keri's hands. "I'll get the other pie out of the oven. Go knead for a while. Maybe pounding on the dough will make you feel better."

With a huff, Keri crossed to the king-size bowl on the table, removed the cover and punched down the risen dough. She grabbed a handful of flour from the canister and slapped it onto the pastry sheet Raven had laid out next to the bowl. Then she tossed the dough into a patch of flour. The white powder flew up and clouded the air around her, then settled wherever it pleased—namely on Keri's jeans and her favorite green shirt. "Great!" Keri groused and attacked the dough.

"For crying out loud, Keri. What's going on with you?" Raven settled into a chair with a mug of hot chocolate and stared up at Keri.

Keri scowled. "Don't you have work to do?" Irritation dripped from her lips, but Raven either didn't notice or, for once, chose not to take up the challenge.

"Nope. I don't have one thing to do at the moment but sip and listen. I just put the apple pie into the oven. Ruth is lying down for her nap, thank goodness, and I'm free as a bird until the pie's done. So stop snapping at me and tell me what happened in the last four hours that's gotten you so riled up. My guess is that it has something to do with Tall, Dark and Handsome. But that's just a hunch." With a smug grin, she leaned the chair back on two legs and took a swig of the hot chocolate. Keri was tempted to give her the same trip to the floor she'd given Justin the night before, but as much as she'd relish the sight of her perfect sister sprawled on the floor, wondering what had hit her, Keri wasn't quite that far gone.

Raven's eyes narrowed and she gave Keri a studied gaze, as though looking for a crack in her armor. Keri stiffened under the appraisal, defenses alerted. Raven knew how to draw information out of people. That was her job and she hadn't gotten where she was without being a student of human nature. But Keri wasn't sure she needed to be interrogated by a reporter. She needed a sympathetic ear. A friend. A sister. Too bad Denni wouldn't arrive at the cabin until tomorrow.

"Leave it alone, Raven." She punched the dough one more time and folded it over. "This is ready. What are we making out of it? Loaves or rolls?"

"Ruth said Dad wants crescent rolls." Raven sniffed. "Do you know how to make those?"

"Nope. Do you?"

A scowl crossed Raven's smooth, dark features. Her chair made a thud as she dropped it to all four legs. "I suppose we'll have to go wake her up, then."

"What's your problem with Ruth, anyway?" Keri asked, relieved the focus of the conversation was focused elsewhere, at least temporarily. "She makes Dad really happy. Something you'd know if you ever showed up."

"Don't start." Raven's voice held an edge of warning to it. "I have my reasons for not coming home, and believe me, you don't want to hear about them."

She was wrong about that, but Keri didn't push. The two had never been that close—not the way they each were to Denni. "All right. I'm sorry. No sniping. Deal?"

Raven smiled and stood. "Thanks. It's a deal. And I won't press you about Justin's case until you're ready to talk about it." She gave Keri a one-armed hug, pressing their cheeks together. "But I promise you, all I want is to help. And I honestly believe I could at least gather facts together. I have Eugene at KCPD. We might be able to get some information that even Justin's lawyer can't pull off."

Pulling away, Keri peered at Raven. "How reliable is this Eugene?"

Raven shrugged. "We dated for a few months." She dropped her arm and cleared her throat.

A groan escaped Keri. She left the dough on the table and moved to the sink to wash her hands. "How reliable is a man whose heart you crushed up and stomped on?"

"Hey! Who said *I'm* the one who ended things?"

Keri sent her a dubious scowl. "You expect me to believe he broke things off with you?" Men just didn't do that to Raven. Her black hair and dark eyes gave her an exotic appeal that guys couldn't seem to get enough of. The aloof, standoffish air she exuded seemed to serve just the opposite of the intended effect. And her trim figure only upped the ante. No. He definitely hadn't broken up with Raven.

Raven sent her a sheepish grin. "Oh, all right, I broke it off, but we've remained friends. I promise. No grudges."

"Sure. No grudges on your part. He probably has a

candlelit shrine built to you in his basement. Thanks anyway, Rave. I think we'll have to pass on your excellent source."

"No need to be sarcastic. I'm just trying to be a good sister and friend and use my resources to clear an innocent man."

Unbidden, a short laugh flew from Keri's lips. Then she cringed, knowing there was no way Raven could let that pass.

"You think he's guilty?" Raven's voice rose a pitch in incredulity, and she put her hand on Keri's, turning her none too gently to face her. "You can stand there and honestly tell me you think that man in there sitting with Dad and holding his sick son in his lap is a murderer? Are you crazy? Where are your cop instincts?"

Keri's temper flared. "How many times do I have to tell you people that it isn't my job to decide whether or not he's guilty? I don't want him to be a killer. But it's not my decision."

"You know what I think? I think you're fighting your feelings for him so hard that you can't see straight. I think you're falling in love all over again—with Justin and with those boys he brought with him."

Tears sprang into Keri's eyes. "Maybe. But it doesn't change anything, Rave."

Raven dismissed her with an airy wave. "Give me a break."

"Hey, in your line of work, you have the luxury of breaking a few rules and it only makes you better, more respected. If I break the rules, I'll lose my job and very likely spend time in jail for obstruction of justice."

"He isn't even charged yet, Kere Bear," Raven said,

reverting to Keri's childhood nickname. "Search your heart, Justin isn't guilty."

"I just wish I could be certain," Keri whispered.

"Work with me. Let's prove it. Let's sit down with Justin tonight. Find out the facts of the case and let me make a couple of phone calls."

The idea had merit. If Raven could help…

"So you agree? We'll sit down with Justin after his boys are in bed tonight?"

Keri nodded. "If Justin agrees."

"Fine. We'll get to the bottom of this and clear Justin in no time." Raven walked toward the kitchen door. "I guess I'll go wake up Ruth so she can make the crescent rolls." Her voice dripped with disdain.

"You should try to get to know her, Rave. I think you'd like her if you gave her a chance."

"I'll think about it." Raven's flip, over-the-shoulder answer pulled a sigh from Keri. She hoped her sister would get over it soon so Dad would set a wedding date.

The roar of Dad's truck motor interrupted her thoughts. Glancing out the window, she frowned as the blue pickup drove down the trail behind the house and into the woods. Surely Dad wouldn't leave the cozy fire to bring up more wood from the pile in the woods. Curiosity drove her into the living room. She stopped short at the sight of Dad, sitting between Josh and Billy—the three of them enraptured by yet another John Wayne Western.

"Hey, Dad. What's Justin doing in the truck?"

"He noticed the woodpile's getting low and offered to drive down and fill up the back of the pickup. Said he had some praying to do and could use the time alone.

With all the unexpected weather, we're going to need the extra wood, anyway."

Praying time? Justin knew every inch of those woods. He knew that four miles along the creek there was a road that would take him away. Nearly dizzy with panic, Keri tried to collect her thoughts.

"Come and watch the movie with the boys and me, Keri-girl."

"Wha—?" she asked distractedly. "Oh. I can't."

She shot through the living room and grabbed her jacket. She fished through the pockets and found her keys.

"Where're you going?" Dad asked, disapproval thickening his tone.

"I'm going to…" She glanced at the boys, then turned a hard gaze on Dad. "I'm going to help Justin with the wood. The snow's starting to come down heavy."

"It is?" With a little squeal, Billy hopped off the couch and ran to the door. He flung it open and stood in awe, staring at the beauty of the fluff falling from the sky. "Hey, look, Josh," he said with a giggle. "The angels have dandruff."

"Grow up," came the weak but obviously disgusted reply. "Are we going to watch this movie or not? It was just getting to the good part."

Billy's face crumpled. Compassion made a trail through Keri's heart. She chucked his chin and smiled down at him. "The angels have dandruff, huh? Maybe we should toss them up some shampoo to take care of that before it's too deep to walk through. You think?"

"Not until it's deep enough to make a snowman, okay?" Billy's attempt to reach past his disappointment in his brother's response and find pleasure in the anticipation of building the snowman further melted Keri's heart.

"Only if you let me help you build it. Deal?" She stuck out her hand.

He took it and grinned. "Deal."

"Okay, back to the movie with you. I need to go and help your dad."

Mac's loud unhappy snort filled the room. "Seems to me when a man says he needs to spend a few minutes alone with his Lord, a person ought to give him the courtesy of letting him do it."

"Sorry, Dad," Keri said, opening the door. "Not this time."

Keri fired up the Jeep, tapping her foot impatiently on the floorboard at the slowness with which it warmed up. Finally she gunned the accelerator and followed Justin's barely discernable tracks. Her pulse quickened as she noticed the blue truck a few hundred yards into the woods. Next to one of the stashes Dad had made this summer. He'd made several stacks of wood in various places on the property so the logs would have a chance to dry out before they needed to burn it. "Nothing starts a flue fire quicker than green wood," Dad insisted. So he'd cut down a dozen trees in an effort to ensure that the only fires at the cabin were the ones he built himself.

Knowing she couldn't park too close or Justin wouldn't be able to turn the truck around, Keri killed the motor fifty yards from where he sat on the wood pile. He didn't turn around as she approached on foot. The truck was running, and Keri could only guess that he hadn't heard the Jeep over the pickup's motor.

As she drew closer, she heard him singing, hands lifted in surrender to his Maker. Recognizing the words, her throat clogged. *"When peace like a river attendeth my way/When sorrow like sea billows roll/Whatever my lot, thou has taught me to say/It is well, it is well with my soul."*

Dad was right. Justin needed time alone with his God. Slowly she backed up, then turned to leave.

"Don't go, Keri," Justin called after her. "Please."

She turned back to face him. "I'm sorry to intrude. Dad said you wanted to pray. I thought—" She dropped her gaze in shame and avoided eye contact as she walked back toward the woodpile. "I—I'm sorry. I just can't seem to keep myself from thinking the worst of you."

Justin rose and met her halfway. "Look at me."

She obeyed his gentle command, tears pushing into her eyes. "You must really hate how suspicious and cynical I've become," she whispered.

Reaching forward, he brushed her cheek with his knuckles. "I could never hate anything about you."

As though of their own volition, her eyes closed at the gentleness of his caress. Warmth engulfed her despite the cold and snow, and she would gladly have stayed out here with him forever.

"Open your eyes."

She met his gaze, warm and in no way condemning.

"You weren't wrong."

"Wrong about what?" Her voice trembled as she voiced the question, unsure she wanted to know the answer.

"I was tempted to keep going and go back to Kansas City."

"What stopped you?"

"You. I couldn't bear the thought of what you might think of me, no matter my reason for going back."

Indignation sprouted in her chest. She plopped her hands onto her hips. "You were just going to leave Billy and Josh?" She couldn't believe it. Not even in her cruelest accusation would she have said Justin would do that, even when faced with the reality that he'd considered it.

He shook his head. "I wasn't leaving for good. Last night Bob told me that someone broke into my house. I want to go home and search the place. Bob thinks it might have been the killer looking for something."

"Was anything taken out of the house that he knows of?"

"Nothing of value for sure. The police think I came home to make it look as though someone broke in. As if that would throw suspicion away from me."

"So what were you planning to do?"

Justin shrugged. "Search for whatever the killer was looking for, I guess. Whatever it was is still there somewhere. If there's anything out of the ordinary, I'm the one who'll find it."

"Raven has some connections in Kansas City. She thinks she might be able to help prove your innocence. I haven't told her much. I don't know much, to be honest. But in any case, I felt you should be the one to tell the story."

"I don't want the boys dragged into the media."

"According to Raven, you've all three been plastered across the TV screens for days."

Justin let out a stiff growl. "I have to prove I didn't

do this thing before they arrest me. It's only a matter of time before the police find out about the cabin. All they'd have to do is talk to Aunt Toni. I'm sure she'd be more than happy to draw them a map."

"You two don't get along?"

He shook his head and gave her a sad smile. "Not really. She tolerated me at best, until I graduated. Then she paid my way into college with the money Mom and Dad had designated for that and told me not to bother coming home on holidays."

Keri dropped the log she was about to toss and pressed a gloved hand to his arm. "Oh, Justin. I'm so sorry."

With a sad half smile, he patted her hand and even through the gloves, Keri felt the electricity of his touch.

"By that time," Justin said, "I knew not to expect any kindness from her. She gave me what she had to and didn't care what I did as long as I didn't interfere in her life."

"That must have been so awful for you. After living the first fourteen years of your life with wonderful parents and friends, to suddenly be all alone… I can't imagine what that must have been like." Her teeth chattered.

Justin's gaze perused her. "Get in the truck and warm up. I can finish this up."

"No way. We'll get done a lot faster if I help. The snow's getting heavier. There has to be a good five inches on the ground as it is. I'll be all right."

He gave a grudging nod. "Okay, but less talking and more tossing. I don't want you getting sick."

She smiled. "I won't."

They tossed wood until the truck bed was filled,

then Keri pulled the Jeep around and took the lead back to the cabin. In the joy of working together with Justin, she had temporarily forgotten that she had to somehow get Josh alone and find out what he knew. Now, that need seemed even more pressing than before.

The pieces of the puzzle somehow didn't fit if Justin had killed Amelia. But what about Josh? The nightmares? The questions? The way he clammed up as soon as Justin came into the room? The fluctuating emotions?

Oh, how she hoped whatever Josh wanted to get off his chest was as simple as catching Billy stealing a comic book or penny gum from a convenience store. But her best instincts told her that whatever was causing his nightmares was linked to the secret he couldn't seem to tell.

Oh, God. Please don't let it be that Justin did this thing. I couldn't bear it.

Chapter Eleven

Justin felt as if he was already on trial. He glanced at the group sitting around the kitchen table. They stared back at him, waiting for him to make them believe in his innocence. A jury of four.

Gathering a slow, unsteady breath, he grabbed his mug, took a swig of bitter decaf, then set it back down. "The police figure she was killed sometime between eleven at night and three in the morning," he said. "Rick had called me around seven and asked me to take his place at the mission because his wife needed him at home."

He had been only too happy to get out of the house that night. News of Amelia's latest fling and the fact that the boys had seen her drunk had thickened the air with tension all day. She was silent and unrepentant, on the defensive, but spoiling for a fight. He was angry the boys had seen her drunk. If not for their housekeeper Mrs. Angus offering to stay the night, he would have turned Rick down for the first time since taking the position as assistant director of the mission. Amelia had already gone to bed when he left, so he knew the boys were in good hands and would be properly cared for in his absence.

"So your relationship with your wife was rocky, to say the least?" Raven's question hung in the air for a moment while Justin tried to decide just how far to go back in the story. Would it really help for them to know about how he came to marry a woman like Amelia in the first place? He glanced at Keri. Her face was drained of color, but she gave him a tremulous smile and a nod.

After wetting his throat with another gulp of coffee, he forged ahead, wishing he had a different story to tell. "You have all known me for so long, except for you, Miss Ruth, and you're practically part of this family. I feel like I should start from when I moved to Kansas City with Aunt Toni."

Ruth gave him a wide sympathetic grin.

"Go ahead, Justin," Keri prompted, her voice tense as though she wasn't sure she really wanted to hear the rest.

Justin smiled, hoping that she would still be able to look at him once she found out how he'd rebelled against God during those years. He glanced from person to person, then focused on a crack in the cup handle. "When I first went to Kansas City, I was determined not to let Aunt Toni's agnostic views affect me. But little by little I slowed down on Bible-reading and devotions.

"Once school started two months after I moved, I made friends who weren't exactly good influences, and before I knew it, I had grown bitter with God for my parents' death. By Christmastime, there wasn't much I hadn't experimented with. Smoking—more than just cigarettes, drinking, even some hard drugs."

He felt the shame churn in his gut. He couldn't face Keri at the next admission. He focused on Mac, instead. "Dating and sex were one and the same for me. I grew numb spiritually and emotionally. I acted without thought."

Silence permeated the room as Justin fast-forwarded through the rest of his pitiful teen years, skipping the details and leaving much to the imagination. "I met Amelia during my sophomore year of college. She got pregnant soon after we met, and I married her."

A low whistle escaped Raven. Justin glanced up at her to find her studying Keri's white face.

Clearing his throat, he knew he had to say something to her. Even if it meant doing so in front of the other three people in the room. "I'm sorry you have to hear this, Keri. But now you see why I didn't come back like I promised. I wasn't the same boy who went away."

Silently, Keri nodded, tears pooling, her lips white and tense.

"Go on, Justin. I think we understand about the beginning of things with your wife." Mac gave him a reassuring nod, and Justin expelled a relieved sigh that there was no anger or condemnation in the wise old eyes.

"Her mom had died a few months before we met, and she had no other family. I was all she had, and she was all I had. Aunt Toni made it pretty clear she wanted nothing to do with me once she considered me grown. So, every month I cashed the check that she sent for my apartment and necessities out of the funds my parents had left me. We had a roommate, too. My aunt paid the school directly so I stayed in college, and Amelia stayed at home, partying all night, sleeping all day. It didn't take long to see we'd made a mistake. But the babies were on the way and I had a responsibility."

Feeling choked, he picked up his coffee cup and glanced inside, only to find it empty. He cleared his throat and set the empty mug back down.

"It was almost unbelievable that she didn't get an abortion. I begged her not to. As soon as the twins were born, she took off with our roommate."

Keri stood, and Justin's heart crashed. She couldn't handle hearing about his disgrace. She'd despise him now. Secure in the knowledge that God had forgiven him long ago, Justin nevertheless had a hard time forgiving himself when he thought of things from her point of view. She'd stayed pure for him while he'd…

He shuddered, then looked up, startled to find her standing over him. She took his cup and walked to the coffeepot, replenished his coffee while no one spoke, and brought it back to him. With a pat on his shoulder and a reassuring, though shaky smile, she gave him an encouraging nod. "Go ahead and finish the story."

Speechless, he met her gaze and the years slipped away. Once again she was the skinny, freckled girl he'd loved as a child, and whom he was beginning to love again. He knew that only God could mend the rift in time, if He so willed.

Grateful for her graciousness, he took a sip of his drink, then picked up where he'd left off.

"I knew I needed to raise the boys in church, so I

found a great one close to home. After about six weeks, Amelia showed up again. She seemed ready to settle down and be a mother, so I let her come back. I figured my sons would be better off with a mother to take care of them, and to be honest, I needed help. So she came back and we picked up where we'd left off, only this time, my relationship with God was slowly being restored. Amelia refused to attend services after a few weeks, and I knew I couldn't force her to live for God. But I was disappointed. My dream was that she would become a Christian, and we could somehow build on that and create the kind of family I had with my mom and dad. I guess she loved the boys as much as she was capable, but she never could quite settle in to motherhood. Before long, she started taking off for days at a time."

"Why'd you keep letting her come back?" Raven stared at him as though she thought he was the worst kind of chump.

Justin felt heat creep up his neck. He shrugged.

"Right after I graduated from college, Rick and his wife started attending my church and we hit it off right away. His wife even tried to befriend Amelia, but, of course, that didn't go anywhere. Anyway, Rick had just taken the position as director of the Victory Mission. It was in shambles. I began volunteering, and, before long, I headed up a volunteer program coordinating people who were willing to cook and serve or wash and mend donated clothing. Within a couple of years, the board was looking for a full-time assistant for Rick.

"I quit my job in sales at a large marketing company

and took this one, for a lot less than I was making. Amelia was furious. But the house was paid for out of the last of the funds my parents had put away for me, plus the life insurance policy. We didn't need fifty-thousand-dollar cars."

Raven raised her brow. "I have to agree with her on that one, Justin. That's a good job to leave to slop tuna casserole on a tray once a day."

"Oh, Raven. Don't be so shallow." Keri's scowl darkened her freckles as she faced her sister. "Of course he had to take the job. Justin has always wanted to help people."

"Oh, he has?" Raven sent her a teasing grin.

Keri's face turned bright red. She cleared her throat. "Does anyone want coffee?"

No one did.

Mac turned back to Justin. "Amelia?"

"Anyway, after the first time she left, our marriage was in name only. She chose that. But I agreed to it happily. The deal was that she wouldn't drink or do drugs around the boys and absolutely no men were allowed in the house. She kept to her end of the deal until the last day."

"All right," Raven said matter-of-factly, glancing up from the notes she'd been jotting. "Let's talk about the day Amelia died."

"Like I said, we really didn't talk all day. The boys told me that they'd seen their mom staggering in while Mrs. Angus was feeding them breakfast. When I got home from my regular overnight at the mission around 11:00 a.m., the boys were in school, of course, and Mrs. Angus filled me in.

"I should have calmed down before going upstairs, but the thought of my boys being forced to see their mother in that condition sent me over the edge. Her door was locked, so I kicked it open."

Mac shook his head. "That didn't make you look innocent, did it?"

Expelling a heavy sigh, Justin shook his head. "No, sir. It didn't."

"What happened next, Justin?" Raven asked.

"Of course, I startled Amelia awake. I remember her being so scared, she screamed and screamed, begging me not to kill her, until I calmed her down, and she realized it was just me."

"So she may have already known someone was out to kill her." Raven's observation took him by surprise.

He shrugged. "Maybe. She was still pretty out of her skull."

"What about your alibi? Surely you have a ton of witnesses who knew you were at the shelter all night."

Justin gazed up at Keri. Apparently she hadn't filled her sister in on too many details. The fact that she'd protected his privacy, even against her sister, or perhaps especially against the reporter, filled him with hope and increased his respect for Keri.

She averted her gaze from him to her sister. "Two residents have come forward who are willing to testify that they saw Justin leave the shelter after lights-out."

"Oh, boy, this isn't going to be easy." Raven leaned forward, frowning in concentration as she wrote something on the pad in front of her. "So the most likely suspect is going to be someone with enough clout to influence a resident at the mission? Your boss?"

Shock zigzagged through Justin with the intensity of lightning. "No way!" He heard the passion in his voice, but didn't care. He knew what it felt like to be wrongfully accused and he couldn't abide the thought of one of his best friends being put in that position.

"Okay, take it easy. It was just a question." Raven rolled her eyes. "We'll keep him off the suspects list for now. Who else had close contact with the residents?"

Justin did a mental checklist. There weren't too many possibilities. "Me. Rick. Bob, my lawyer. He helps out with some pro bono cases. But there again, he's a good friend. Like Rick. There's just no way he could be responsible."

Raven gathered a long breath and let it out slowly. She tapped the end of her pen on the table. "O-kay. Two possible suspects who aren't capable of double-crossing a friend, for whatever reason. Who else then?" She glanced up from the notepad, her brow raised in question.

Mac, Ruth and Keri all turned to him, obviously thinking along the same lines as Raven.

Defenses raised by Raven's sarcasm and the consensus of skepticism, Justin forced himself not to voice his frustration. Instead he searched his memory and picked through a possible list of the volunteers and part-time employees who might have a vendetta against him. He had named three or four possibilities when the kitchen door opened and Billy stumbled in rubbing his eyes.

"What are you doing up, son?" he asked.

"I'm thirsty."

Keri stood. "Follow me, Billy-boy. I'll get you a drink."

Feeling suddenly stifled in the warm kitchen, Justin stood, as well. "I'm going to call it a night. Maybe we can pick this up in the morning."

A wide yawn stretched Mac's mouth. He suffocated it with the back of his veined hand and stood, arching his back. "That's probably for the best," he said. With a cautious glance toward Billy, he dropped his tone. "Thank you for opening up to us, Justin. I'm more convinced than ever that you didn't do this." He sent Keri a pointed look.

Justin stretched out his hand. Mac ignored the offering and pulled him in for a hug instead. "You just keep your hope in the Lord, my boy. He is a God of faithfulness, and He knows you're innocent. Keep looking for a way to prove your innocence." He pulled away and winked. "And don't mind Raven, there. She's naturally suspicious."

"Thanks a lot, Dad," she drawled, rolling her eyes.

A chuckle escaped Justin despite the difficulty of the last hour. "I'll try to remember that." He directed his attention to Billy. "Ready to go back to bed?"

The boy gave a sleepy nod and leaned his head against Justin's waist.

As they stepped out of the kitchen, Justin overheard Keri's husky voice. "So, what do you think, Rave?"

"I think Justin is innocent, but very, very naive." Justin's ears burned as he slowed his steps. "Someone is setting him up, and I'm sure it's one of his friends."

Chapter Twelve

Keri opened her eyes, instantly alert. She glanced over at the glowing numbers on the clock next to her bed and groaned. Four o'clock. Another night of little to no sleep.

Immersed in slumber, Ruth snorted and turned onto her side, pulling the quilts with her. Shivering, Keri eased out of bed, slipped on her fuzzy leopard-spotted slippers, her half-moon-accented terry-cloth robe, and moved into the hallway toward the kitchen for a drink of water.

After two nights of sleeping with Ruth, she was beginning to feel sorry for Dad, and the thought occurred to her that someone might have tipped him off about his fiancée's sleeping habits. Maybe that was the real reason he kept putting off setting the date for the wedding. The woman couldn't be still or quiet while she slept any more than she could while she was awake. A smile lit Keri's face as she pushed open the kitchen door. She loved Ruth, anyway. So maybe she'd keep quiet about it. No sense in giving Dad an excuse to give in to cold feet.

The light above the sink glowed softly into the otherwise dark cabin. Keri frowned. She had been the last person to turn in the night before and she knew she'd switched off that light. Her heart picked up a few beats as anxiety swept her. Could someone be in the cabin? She scowled at the absurdity of the thought. What thief in his right mind would turn on the kitchen light? Relaxing a bit, she nevertheless walked to the back door and rattled the doorknob. It was locked, with no sign that anyone had come in through that avenue.

Keri shook her head at her paranoia. Most likely, she'd forgotten to turn off the light. Either that or someone had gotten up for a drink of water and had simply left it on so they could see their way through the house. In any case, there was no intruder.

She turned on the faucet and filled a glass with the ice-cold water sliding through the pipes. A sigh lifted and lowered her chest and she turned, leaning against the sink. Her gaze swept the kitchen and she could imagine that in just a few hours, the turkey would be tempting everyone in the cabin with its delicious aroma. They would all sit around the large table—after Dad added several mismatched chairs so there would be enough to go around. It had been ages since they'd had a Thanksgiving meal at the cabin. It only seemed right that Justin and the boys were here. After all, the Thanksgiving tradition had always consisted of the Mahoneys and Kramers.

Would the tradition live on? Or with the very real possibility of Justin going to prison and the boys into foster care, was this the last time they'd be together for the holiday? The thought churned Keri's gut, but she pushed aside the dark musing, determined to enjoy today if for no other reason than to give Justin and the boys one last holiday together before his arrest.

She glanced at the clock on the wall. Four-ten. Three more hours of sleep—tops. She'd better go back and hope she was so exhausted even Ruth couldn't keep her awake.

Just as she turned to rinse out her glass, her gaze swept over a slip of white paper left in the center of the counter, next to the coffeepot. Frowning, Keri lifted the note, then gasped as she read.

> Keri,
> I have to know what the killer is after. Mrs. Angus scared him off the first time, but it stands to reason he'll be back. I want to get there first if it isn't too late already. I plan to be back by the end of the day with good news. If for some reason I don't return, please know how badly I regret the way my life unfolded. And despite my love for my boys, my biggest mistake was not coming back for you. You turned out to be everything a man could ask for in a woman. I won't make the same mistake twice. If at all possible, I'm coming back for you this time.
>
> Justin.

Keri's eyes burned as she read and reread the note with tear-blurred vision. He regretted not coming back for her. That meant he still cared. Just as she did.

"Justin," she whispered. What was he doing going off looking for clues all alone?

He was doing exactly what she would do if her life and the lives of her children were at stake. The difference was that she was trained for it. He wasn't. And what kind of woman let the man she loved face a dangerous, unknown enemy alone? Definitely not her.

Moments later, fully dressed, she made her way through the living room, listening to her dad's even breathing from his makeshift bed on the couch.

Raven slept, mouth open, in front of the fireplace. Keri grinned. Too bad she didn't have a camera handy. That picture would be worth a million bucks—or could serve as a nice consolation token for every poor sap Raven threw over for no good reason.

Raven stirred, then opened her eyes. "Kere Bear?"

"Shh. Go back to sleep."

The last thing Keri needed was for her sister to wake up and start asking questions. She inwardly cringed as Raven rose up on her elbow and stared at her, the glow from the small flame in the fireplace dancing across her perfect skin. "What time is it? And why are you all dressed? Where are you going?"

Why couldn't Raven have chosen a career in medicine? She always asked the right questions. Nothing got past her and for the first time ever, Keri wished her sister was a lousy reporter instead of such an ace.

"Justin took off for Kansas City to try to look for some clues in his house. Something the killer might have left behind."

"After all this time?" Raven sat up the rest of the way and hugged her knees to her chest. "The detectives would have swept that place long ago and taken anything relevant."

"Yes. But Justin's lawyer said the place was broken into a couple of nights ago."

Even in just the glow from the firelight, Keri could see the interest spark in Raven's eye. "The killer came back to the scene," Raven said, excitement building in her words. "You know what that means?"

"Obviously he left something to incriminate himself."

"And to prove Justin's innocence." She jumped to her feet. "I'm getting dressed. Wait for me. I want to come, too."

"No way. I'm not taking you away from Dad on the first Thanksgiving you've been here in five years."

Raven hesitated as though weighing her words. Releasing a heavy sigh, she nodded. "I guess you're right."

"Neither one of you ought to be going out in this weather."

They both turned to the sound of Mac's voice.

"Sorry for waking you, Dad." Keri walked to the rack and grabbed her coat. "Justin took off for Kansas City and I'm going after him."

Sitting up in the dark, Mac switched on the lamp next to the couch. "Leave him be to do what he has to do, Keri."

"I'm not going after him to force him back," she said, exasperation thick in her voice. "I might be able to help. I imagine he's going to search his house. I plan to go straight to the mission and nose around. If I find anything I'll call his cell phone."

He nodded. "All right, then. Be looking for my truck. That's what he's driving."

"Dad! You knew he was going and didn't say anything?"

Looking rather pleased with himself, Mac grinned.

"That's right. Justin tiptoed in here around midnight. He planned to drive his own car in all this mess. I told him he wouldn't get to the highway in that car of his and tossed him the keys to my truck. That four-wheel drive will go anywhere."

Keri glanced at her glowing watch. "So he's been on the road almost five hours. As slowly as he'll be driving, he's probably either not there yet, or just getting there."

Raven nodded. "It took me four and a half hours yesterday and that was with most of the main roads in fair shape. With the snow ending around seven last night, the road crews should have been out clearing and laying down salt. The little highway will be the most dangerous, Kere Bear. So take it easy."

An uncharacteristic surge of affection shot through Keri for her sister. She grabbed Raven and pulled her close for a snug embrace.

Raven returned the hug, then pressed a quick kiss to her cheek. "Justin's worth this," she whispered. "And so are those precious boys. You're doing the right thing."

Keri pulled away and looked from her dad to her sister. "Pray."

Though dawn was beginning to glimmer through the ice-laden branches lining Justin's street, there was just enough of the grayness left to cloak him while he unlocked the back door and entered his home. First he checked all the curtains and blinds to be sure no one could see inside and catch him moving around. Then he stood in the center of the living room for a moment, savoring the sights and smells of his home. Amazing how despite the circumstances, he felt a sense of comfort just in coming home.

What would it have been like if he'd have come home after work and Keri had been the one to greet him every day? He climbed the stairs, swept away in a dream of redheaded babies and growing old with his childhood sweetheart.

Reality bit him hard when he reached the landing and found the door to Amelia's room wide open. The intruder had definitely been the killer, or at least in some way involved in Amelia's death.

Justin had made a point of closing the door and leaving it that way after the last time the police had been in here. He'd finally been given permission to replace the frame that had shattered when he kicked the door open that day. The police had taken plenty of photos.

After Amelia's death, he'd had every intention of selling the house and moving to another neighborhood in the boys' school district. Someplace they wouldn't have to remember their mother's drunken staggering. Where they could walk past the living room and not imagine their mother's dead body. But once he'd become chief suspect, Bob had warned him against the idea. Could look bad for the grieving widower to sell the house so soon after his wife's death.

The police knew the truth about the marriage, but a prosecutor might put an ugly spin on the situation and make the jury question the selling of the house.

The first thing he planned to do upon clearing his name was put the house on the market.

Gathering a long, slow breath, he stepped through the door to Amelia's room. As much as he hated walking inside, he knew his answers most likely lay within those four walls. He glanced around at the Santa Fe decor. The one thing Amelia hadn't lacked was an eye for design, and she enjoyed the Southwestern, native-American look. Navajo Indian pottery was all over the place, from the three-foot-high vase in the corner filled with dried plants, weeds as far as Justin was concerned, to the matching lamp on the nightstand.

Justin took another look at the vase. Probably too obvious a place to hide anything and he wouldn't be the only person who'd thought to look. He shrugged and headed for the corner, anyway. It couldn't hurt to check it out just in case.

"Oh, no you don't!"

Startled, Justin spun around just as his head exploded with pain.

Once Keri left the secluded highway leading to the cabin, the roads looked much better and she was able to accelerate, almost matching the speed limit. She reached the city by nine and took the first promising exit with a gas station that didn't look too run-down from the interstate. The phone book was missing from the pay phone, so she went inside, wishing for all she was worth that she hadn't insisted on no cell phones on what was supposed to have been their vacation.

She grabbed a bottle of water and a donut, then went to the counter.

"Do you have a phone book handy?" She asked giving the middle-aged, ponytailed man behind the counter her nicest grin. He grunted and reached under the counter. Defenses on full alert, Keri watched his tattooed hand pull out a four-inch-thick book. He dropped it on the counter. "Two-fifty."

"To use the phone book?"

He gave her a lopsided grin, making him appear less gruff. "The water and donut."

"Oh. Sorry." Keri pulled three dollar bills from her pocket and handed them to him. "Long night."

"You in town for Thanksgiving?"

"Something like that," Keri mumbled as she perused the residential pages. Panic began to flood through her. Justin's name wasn't there. "Is this a current book?"

"Yep."

Her shoulders slumped as she closed the book. Then an idea glimmered and she opened to the Yellow Pages.

"I'm pretty familiar with the city. Maybe I can help."

"Thanks, I found it." She memorized the number, smiled back at the man and headed back outside.

She gripped the receiver with two fingers and grimaced at the thought of how many germs were most likely lurking on the thing. She got through on the first ring. A man's voice answered. "Victory Mission, Happy Thanksgiving. Rick speaking."

"Yes, hello. This is Keri Mahoney."

She rolled her eyes. This is Keri Mahoney? Like that was going to make an impression on him.

"I'm sorry, who?"

"Uh—actually, I'm a friend of Justin Kramer's. I was wondering if you could tell me how to get to the mission."

"I'm sorry, but Justin isn't here today." His voice sounded wary.

"Yes, I know. I'm—look I'd rather not go into this

over the phone. Will you please give me directions?" She told him which exit she'd taken. "I need to get over there."

"Any cabbie in the city knows where the mission is located," he said.

"A cab?" Keri wasn't sure she liked this Rick guy, even if he was Justin's best friend. "Look, I am driving my own vehicle. I need directions, not advice about cabs."

"I know you say you're a friend of Justin's, and I'm sure you are, but I've got several hundred guests lining up to eat turkeys that aren't even finished cooking yet. I'm short on volunteers and my help is desperately needed. You have the address. There is no point in my giving you directions because there's no place to park anywhere near the place. And if you did park you wouldn't have a car when you went out to find it. I hope you'll take that cab and come down, we could use the help today."

Keri stared at the silent receiver, then hung it up. Now what? With a huff, she stomped back into the store. The biker-type clerk gave her another grin and pulled the phone book out. "Need this again?"

"Can I leave my Jeep here for a few hours while I go to the Victory Mission? I was just informed there's no place to park."

He narrowed his gaze. "What do you want to go down there for, anyway?"

Tempted to tell him that was none of his business, Keri studied him for a second and changed her mind. He didn't look like the kind of guy you'd want to anger. "They're shorthanded on volunteers to help serve Thanksgiving dinner. I thought I'd go down and pitch in."

Apparently, that was the right thing to say, because the tall, ponytailed biker boy smiled, his eyes kind. "Let me call a cab for you. I'll make sure no one messes with your Jeep."

Keri wasn't sure whether to trust him or not. While her head and all of her training screamed at her not to be stupid, her best instincts told her he was on the level. And what other choice did she really have?

"Thanks. I'd appreciate it. What time do you get off work? I don't want to take a chance the guy coming into work after you might not be so generous."

Picking up the phone, he dialed a number from memory. "Today's your lucky day, then. I'm working a double shift."

"On Thanksgiving?"

"Yep."

"But you'll miss out on your family dinner."

He nodded. "So will you." Then he raised his hand, cutting off her reply. "Hi, Tina? Yeah, it's Mike. Look, I need a cab over here to go down to the Victory Mission. How soon can you send someone over? Uh—no. Don't send Ken. I think the lady would be more comfortable with Rob. Do you mind?"

Keri watched him in fascination. Despite his outward appearance, this Mike guy seemed as nice as they came. He hung up the phone and nodded. "Rob'll be here in a few minutes."

"Thanks. I'll just go lock up the Jeep."

Keri used the extra time to place a calling-card call to her dad's cell phone.

"Hi, Ruth," she said when the woman's soft drawl answered.

"Where are you, Keri, honey?"

"I made it to Kansas City and I'm about to head over to the mission. I'm waiting for my cab."

"Cab? Did your Jeep break down?"

"No. I—"

"Hold on, Keri. Your dad wants to speak to you."

"What's this about your Jeep breaking down? What's it doing? Do I need to come and get you?"

"Dad, no. Everything's fine. It's just that there is no place to safely park close to the mission, so I'm parking here and taking a cab."

"Parking where? What do you mean? Didn't you find Justin?"

Thankfully, Keri saw a yellow cab pull into the parking lot. As it honked, she said, "Sorry, Dad. I have to go. I'll call you a little later. Don't worry!"

Hurrying over to the cab, Keri waved to Mike through the glass door. He returned the wave and smiled.

"Hi," she said as she slipped into the back seat. "Can you take me to the Victory Mission?"

"Sure can." He moved to the edge of the parking lot, then gunned the accelerator, screeching into the thickening traffic. "Is that how you know Mike?"

"I don't know him. He just offered to keep an eye on my car today."

The cabbie nodded, but didn't say any more.

Keri sucked in her breath as the cabbie sailed through a light turning from yellow to red.

"Why'd you think I'd met him at the Mission?"

"Mike used to stay there a lot back in his drinking days. Before he found the Lord."

"Oh?"

"Yep. Got drunk one time and ran his car head-on into a concrete underpass wall. Killed his wife and baby daughter instantly. Poor guy walked away with barely a scratch."

"Well, wasn't he the lucky one?"

"Believe me, he paid for it. They gave him a few years in jail, and when he got out, he just couldn't live with himself. Took to drinking again and ended up on the streets. Hit all the missions and shelters. But Victory Mission is where he got straightened out."

"Well, I suppose that's good." Feeling ill, Keri stared out the window, watching as the buildings grew less and less cared for, the streets dirtier the deeper they drove into the city. Finally, they pulled up in front of a doorway with a painting above it of a large dove carrying a branch and the words, Victory Mission. Ask Us About New Beginnings.

"I'd walk you in," he said. "But my cab wouldn't be here when I came out."

Fishing for the fare, Keri waved away his apology. "I'm a cop. I can take care of myself."

"That's a pretty rough-looking mob out there."

Keri followed his gaze and swallowed hard. "Yeah." They were lined along the building and crowded on the sidewalk all the way to the street. Men, women and children in tattered clothing, trying to push their way into the mission. Would she even be able to get in?

"Tell you what. I'll stay here until you get inside. Will that help?"

"Maybe." She took out an extra five and added it to the cash still in her hand. When she extended it, he shook his head. "This trip is on Mike."

"No way. Take it."

"Would you have accepted the trip from Mike before you found out what happened to his wife and baby?"

The cold accusation in the cabbie's voice chilled Keri to her bones. Would she have?

"If you can't accept his way of saying thanks for giving your time to help out down here today, then just donate the money once you get inside. But I'm not taking it."

"Let me ask you something," Keri said, on the defensive now. "If Mike is so generous, why isn't he down here serving food himself?"

"First off, because the man he's covering for at the gas station has a family, and Mike insisted on working all sixteen hours today so that his fellow employee wouldn't miss out on Thanksgiving. Second, Mike has nowhere to go but home to an empty apartment."

"All right," Keri muttered. "Mike's a saint." She tucked the money back into her pocket. "I'll donate it."

"Do you care about the other reason Mike doesn't come down here and volunteer?"

"Yeah, sure."

"Because he knows that even with the Lord, he is weak. He doesn't feel strong enough to be down here with the men who once drank with him. He knows he could wind up right back in the gutter if he isn't careful. So he sends donations, and prays and hopes for the day when he can be of service."

Tears pushed into Keri's eyes. She blinked them away and swallowed hard. "Okay. I better go inside or I won't be any help today, either. Thanks for the lift."

Keri hurried from the cab, not sure which she preferred, the gauntlet of catcalls, wolf whistles and lewd suggestions, or the conviction that had closed in on her as she sat listening to the cabbie telling her of a broken, but changed man.

She got inside without being accosted, and a cafeteria-style room greeted her. Tables were spread with white paper tablecloths and every attempt had been made to make the "guests" comfortable, including horns-of-plenty centerpieces and real dishes, rather than paper plates and plastic cups.

The line stretched the length of the crowded room. Keri made her way to the front. "Hey, get in line, sweet cheeks."

A rough hand grabbed her arm and spun Keri around. A woman's icy, brown-eyed glare met her. She had to be fifty if she was a day and she wore a wide-brimmed straw hat decorated with sunflowers.

"I'm sorry. I'm here to help, not eat."

The woman squinted, clearly accusing her of lying. "Never seen you here before."

A crowd was beginning to form around them.

"Clean her clock, Auntie Em!"

"Kick her to the back of the line."

Keri's heart picked up speed. One Auntie Em she could definitely handle, but several members of the crowd were looking a little too eager to join the fight.

"Now, look," she said, fixing her steely gaze on the still-gathering crowd. "I didn't come down here to cut in line. That doesn't even make sense. I'm just here to—"

"All right. Break it up." The crowd parted in response to a deep, loud voice. The voice of authority. Keri looked up. Way up. The man was at least six foot four and dressed in jeans and a T-shirt. Stern blue eyes censured her through wire-rimmed glasses. "What do you want?"

"See, I told ya she wasn't here to help out. Rick don't even know her."

"Oh, so you're Rick?" Relief nearly weakened her knees. "I'm Keri. Justin's friend. We spoke on the phone earlier."

"I'm afraid I still don't have time to talk. You see this line? These people are waiting for a Thanksgiving meal."

"I know. You told me over the phone that you're short on volunteers. Right?" Keri followed him back to the serving line. A half a dozen people worked feverishly, serving, adding food to the serving bins and scraping dishes and loading washers.

"Yeah. Fine. We can use an extra pair of hands." He tossed her an apron. "Put this on."

Keri slipped the apron over her head and wrapped and tied the strings. "Okay. What should I do?"

Rick gestured over the entire kitchen area. "Whatsoever your hands find to do, do with all your heart as unto the Lord."

Keri grinned and took a look at the huge pile of dirty trays. "Gotcha."

Chapter Thirteen

Justin fought through smoky confusion and struggled to open his eyes. A dull ache began at the base of his head and radiated around to his brow. He moaned as light stabbed his eye sockets, giving a whole new meaning to the word *pain*. Squeezing his eyes tight, he sat up.

"Oh, Justin. I'm so glad you're awake. I was about to call an ambulance."

Turning to the sound of the woman's voice, Justin opened his eyes slowly, ready to shut them again if the searing pain returned. But it was bearable.

"Mrs. Angus? What are you doing here?" The fifty-something housekeeper sat next to him on the bed.

"Let me see that bump," she commanded. Justin leaned his neck way over to accommodate her.

"What happened?" Justin asked, fully aware the woman hadn't yet answered the first question.

"You've got a goose egg, that's for sure," she mumbled and turned him loose. She sighed deeply. "After the house was broken into, I decided I'd better stay for a few days to see if the snake returned. I didn't recognize you from behind. It was dark and I thought you were the killer coming back."

A surge of affection shot through Justin. He took her hands in his. "I appreciate that you want to help clear my name, but you could have gotten yourself hurt. What if I'd actually been the murderer?"

She snorted. "Then you'd be sitting in a jail cell right now, nursing a knot on the head."

"That's not the point." Knowing there was no sense in continuing this line of conversation, Justin glanced around, looking for a clock. "What time is it?"

"Going on eleven."

"Eleven!" Justin shot to his feet, but a wave of dizziness sent him back to the bed. "What did you hit me with?"

"Skillet."

"Must have been the biggest one in the house. I've lost hours of searching."

The dear woman's face drooped a bit.

Justin squeezed her hand. "Mrs. Angus, I appreciate that you want to help, but you've done all you can. I want you to go home, okay? Didn't your daughter come in from Nebraska for Thanksgiving?"

She shook her graying head. "I told her not to this year. See, I think the killer will expect everyone to be busy today. He most likely figures he can get over here unnoticed to find what he's looking for. I decided to hide out and try to catch him. Like the *Murder, She Wrote* woman."

"Well, I'm glad it was me and not the killer who surprised you." Releasing a heavy sigh, Justin rose again, slowly this time. "I just wish I knew what he thinks is here that will incriminate him. Whatever it is will probably clear me. Unless he actually did find it when he broke in. In which case, I'm probably sunk."

The housekeeper hesitated a moment, then stood. "I'll be right back."

Justin frowned after her. He reached back and felt the knot on his head, then grimaced. Too bad he hadn't been the bad guy. Mrs. Angus packed quite a wallop.

His mind wandered back to the little cabin and he thought about his sons waiting for the turkey to finish cooking. For the past two years they'd helped at the mission, and in previous years, Mrs. Angus had brought leftover turkey to the house, but they'd never actually experienced the kind of family Thanksgiving dinner they were about to experience today. If only he could have been there to witness the fun and wonder.

He was positive Keri would be sure they got to split the wishbone. He smiled, remembering all the ones he and Keri had split over the years. The wishes they'd made. From their very first time, he and Keri had secretly agreed to wish for the same thing. That way no matter who won, the wish came true. It had been his idea. They wished they'd be friends forever. After they'd fallen in love, they began to wish separately. But Justin's always remained the same—with a slight twist. That he and Keri would be together forever. Too bad he'd lost the last wishbone pull they had together the Thanksgiving before his parents had been killed.

What were the boys thinking right now? How were they coping with his absence? He'd kissed them each on the head and left a note to reassure them he'd be back soon. Still, he had a feeling they might feel abandoned. Especially on the holiday. They had the family though. Keri, Mac, Ruth and even Raven.

As he waited for Mrs. Angus to return and tried to get his bearings, he replayed the conversation he'd had with Mac before leaving this morning.

"If I don't come back, will you consider keeping my sons? Raising them, I mean."

Mac hadn't hesitated. Hadn't tried to give him any trite reassurances that everything would be okay. He'd simply leveled his wizened gaze upon him. "I'll do it. And you can count on it."

Justin had penned his wishes on a legal pad, knowing it probably wouldn't stick in court if anyone contested Mac's right to custody. But he also knew there was no one who would care. The simple act of signing his name and having Mac sign underneath in his shaky hand had given Justin a huge sense of peace. If nothing else went his way, at least the boys would be loved and safe and not in foster care.

"I think this may be what the killer was looking for." Mrs. Angus's return to the room brought Justin back to the present. She handed him a fat spiral notebook.

"What's this?"

"Amelia used this to keep a diary of sorts. I found it under Josh's toy box. Don't ask me why it was in there. Makes no sense to me."

"What were you doing looking through Josh's toy box?"

"Cleaning. I had to do something with my time. When I lifted it up to vacuum underneath, this fell out of the bottom, like it had been stashed there for safekeeping."

The room was starting to spin again, so Justin took the notebook and sat back down on the edge of the bed.

"Read July fifteenth," Mrs. Angus said, taking the chair next to the window. "It's the last entry."

"Don't you think solving the mystery by reading a diary is just a little too Hollywood?" he asked, thumbing through the pages until he found the entry.

July fifteenth. Two days before her death.

Josh heard us talking on the phone. I yelled at him when I caught him hiding behind the chair, listening. He ran away, but not before hearing me telling HIM I'm pregnant. What am I going to do? I have to convince Josh not to tell Justin. What a *mess*! Why can't anything ever go right for me??? A baby seemed like a good idea, but now I'm not so sure I can pull it off. *HE* suggested I give the baby to his wife.

Justin sucked in his breath, shaking his head.

"Read the part about Amelia being pregnant?"

"Yeah." He read the passage again, frowning. "Josh has been carrying this secret around with him for months. What could she have said to him that he wouldn't have told me? Especially after she died?"

"The poor boy. That woman was no mother if you ask me!"

"I don't think anyone could dispute that. But one thing I can't understand about this is that if she was pregnant, wouldn't the autopsy have shown something? Why didn't the police mention it?"

"Maybe they just didn't tell you. Figured you should already know since she was your wife."

Justin gave a short laugh. "Believe me, if Raney and Appling knew anything about it, they'd have used her pregnancy to rub me raw. They know we didn't share a bed."

"Hmm. Do you think she was lying?" Mrs. Angus gave him a pointed glance. "You know, some women do that to try to force a man into marriage."

Justin scowled. "She didn't lie to me about being pregnant before we were married."

Her cheeks reddened. "I didn't say she did. Just that I wouldn't put it past her to say she was."

Releasing a heavy sigh, Justin nodded. "Well, one thing is pretty clear. This could raise some questions for the detectives. It shows that someone besides me had motive to kill her. I'd better let Bob know." He reached for the phone next to Amelia's bed, then pulled away.

Justin scrubbed his hand over his scratchy jaw. He hadn't taken time to shave before leaving the cabin and the stubble was beginning to irritate. "I'm sure the police bugged Bob's phone the second they found out I took off. I'm going to have to drive over there."

Keri spooned gravy over a mound of mashed potatoes. She made a point of looking the young woman she was serving in the eye. Rick had instructed her that making eye contact raised a person's dignity. She went a step further and smiled.

"Thank you." The young woman's voice sounded weary. The obviously pregnant mother carried an infant of no more than a year old on her hip, while two preschool-aged boys clamored around her legs, chasing each other and jostling their poor mother.

Keri felt like grabbing them up, carrying them over to a couple of chairs, and instructing them to be still—even if she had to use her cop status to scare them into submission. But she knew that wasn't her place. Instead, she filled two trays for the boys. "Here, let me carry these to a table for you."

Relief softened the tense lines around the young woman's mouth, and Keri saw the hint of a smile.

Keri set both trays in front of the boys, then turned to their mother. "I'm Keri." She stretched out her hand. The woman wiped her palm on her age-faded jeans before accepting Keri's.

"I'm Erin." She smiled wider. Her teeth were black from cavities, and Keri's heart melted in sympathy.

"It's nice to meet you, Erin. Happy Thanksgiving."

"Thank you." Erin's gaze dropped to the table and she lifted a forkful of potatoes to the baby's mouth. Keri focused on the two little boys. They were already half-finished with their food. How long had it been since they'd eaten a decent meal? Tears spilled over as she walked back to resume her spot in the serving line. How could she have lived twenty-nine years and never been witness to this kind of human suffering?

"You can serve the people without it destroying you." Keri glanced up to find Rick had moved to her side. "Come on, we'll trade places with Kim and wash dishes for a while. You don't want to let them see you cry. It puts some of them on the defensive. And the others will see you as weak and con you into giving up all your money."

Keri nodded and followed Rick to the back of the kitchen area. She attacked the pile of dirty dishes, fighting desperately to control her emotions. "I'm sorry," she said, snatching a couple of tissues from a box Rick offered.

"We can't fulfill every need. All we can do for now is serve one meal a day and pray for their souls. We have room for about fifty residents a night in the men's shelter."

"But what about the women and children?"

"We do what we can. We're only staffed for men. But there are other missions and shelters. And government programs help women and children first."

"It just seems so unfair and awful that children should have to trudge out in the snow for a meal."

"But if we weren't here, they'd sit at home hungry. If they even have a home. So at least we do some good." Rick nodded toward Erin. "Take that woman and her children, for instance. They come here every day. And even though we can't offer them a place to stay, we can at least feed them one hot meal a day."

"But where do they sleep at night, I wonder?"

"Maybe a low-rent apartment. Or shelters here and there."

"She's pregnant. Do you think she's getting prenatal care?"

"I doubt it. But what can we do?"

"Open a home for women and children. Or at least a shelter."

"We do the best we can do."

"I'm sure it must be difficult to see this sort of poverty day in and day out."

He heaved a heavy sigh and moved away. Keri's gaze followed his retreating form. Rick seemed all right, but a little burned-out and perhaps ready for a sabbatical.

Justin would be the logical replacement. Keri couldn't help but picture him in the middle of the crowd, ministering. What would it have been like if they'd entered this ministry together? She envisioned herself working with him side by side to feed the needy.

Somehow, the vision stayed with her over the next two hours as she spooned the Thanksgiving meal onto tray after tray. Finally, Rick announced there was nothing left and closed the doors amid cries of protest.

Keri glanced around at the faces of the people who had given so tirelessly of their time over the past few hours, wonderful people with whom she'd worked side by side. The pain in their eyes reflected the heaviness of her heart.

Rick leaned against the counter. "There's never enough to go around. We could serve around the clock and they'd still be standing out there begging for more. We can only do so much. And we do."

Keri frowned. There might not be anything they could do, but he didn't have to be so matter of fact about it.

As though reading her thoughts, he narrowed his gaze and gave a short laugh. "Think whatever you want, but ask Justin what it's like to work down here day after day with people who constantly ask for what we don't have to give."

"I know Justin," Keri said, suddenly angry. "He doesn't feel that way. He can't wait to get back here and—"

"You've been in recent contact with Justin?" Rick's

eyes narrowed. He wrapped his massive hand around her upper arm. "Come on. Let's go talk in my office."

"Excuse me." A man dressed in a sport jacket and navy slacks interrupted, his attention focused on Rick. The man's face was lined with evidence of a hard life, but his eyes bespoke joy, contentment.

"What can I do for you?" Rick asked, clearly irritated, but he turned Keri loose.

"I'm looking for Justin. I thought he'd be here for the dinner today."

"Justin had other things to do today."

The man's expression crashed. "Well, can you give him a message for me?"

"I don't know when we'll see him again. He left town."

"I see. Well, if you see or hear from him, will you tell him Ike Rawlings was by? I thought Thanksgiving would be a good day to tell him how thankful I am for all his help. We came all the way from Chicago to tell him in person. He smiled at Keri. "I left my wife back at the hotel so she could rest. She just found out we're going to have our fourth baby."

Keri returned his smile. "Congratulations."

"Thanks. God restored my family to me and is giving me a brand-new start to be the kind of father I should have been to the other three. He used Justin to save me and dry me out. I just wanted to thank him and show him it stuck."

"I'll tell him," Keri said softly. She reached out and touched the man's arm. "I know he'll be thrilled with your news. If you'll write down your address and phone number, I'll be sure to give it to him."

"You know where he is?" Rick asked.

Covering quickly, Keri refrained from meeting Rick's direct gaze. "I meant I would give him the information when I see him."

"Just give him this." Ike reached into his jacket pocket and produced a business card. He beamed. "I run my own business now, cleaning carpets and drapes."

His enthusiasm was infectious and Keri couldn't keep from grinning. "If I ever need my carpets or drapes cleaned I'll give you a call. Do you travel?"

A twinkle lit his eyes. "For a friend of Justin's? You bet." He turned to Rick. "Do you mind if I stay and talk to some of the men sleeping in the residence hall tonight?"

"I think that's a great idea."

Keri glanced at Rick, surprised at his enthusiasm. This Ike was the real McCoy. A testimony to Justin's calling. She took pleasure in the thought of his face when she produced the card and told him Ike was about to be a father again. This would be welcome news in Justin's overwhelmingly disappointing life right now.

"It was nice to meet you, Ike," Keri said as he said goodbye and left the cafeteria. He disappeared through a door off the dining area, leaving Keri open for the one question she didn't want to answer.

"Where's Justin?"

Bob's brow rose in surprise when he answered Justin's knock. "Come in!" he said, stepping out of the way. "When did you get back in town? I haven't heard anything about a warrant."

Justin entered the spacious one-level frame home. The smell of turkey and dressing filled the air with luscious scents, making him long for the boys, who were undoubtedly about to sit down to a Thanksgiving dinner with the Mahoneys. "I came back to find whatever the killer was looking for at my house. And I think I might have found it."

A frown creased Bob's brow. "What do you mean?"

He lifted the notebook for Bob's perusal.

The lawyer gave it a once-over then glanced back at Justin, brow raised in question. "What's this?"

"Amelia's diary."

"I didn't know she kept one."

"How would you? I didn't even know. And she was my wife."

"I just figured if she'd have had a diary, the police would have discovered it. What's in there that might help?"

"She claimed to be pregnant. Was talking on the phone to the baby's father when Josh overheard the whole thing."

"Josh?" Bob's face drained of color. "You're saying he heard her tell the baby's father she was pregnant?"

"Yes. I think this might have something to do with why he's having nightmares about the killer and why his behavior has changed so drastically since Amelia's death."

Justin offered him the diary. "The fact that she was pregnant could cast light on another suspect. The guy she was seeing was married, so that alone might cause him to commit murder."

"Interesting theory." Bob took the notebook and tucked it under his arm. "Can I keep this? I'd like to read it thoroughly and see if I can come up with anything that might help clear you. Maybe she slipped in a name or something."

"Keep it. I hope you'll find something helpful. I thought you might want to take it to the police. At least they'd know there was someone else out there with motive."

Bob nodded. "Good thinking. I'll call Appling in the morning and let him know we have it." He motioned toward the dining room. "We're just about to sit down and eat. Would you like to join us?"

Justin studied his friend's face. Tension lined his features and a muscle twitched in his jaw. "Is everything okay?"

Bob shrugged. "I forgot to pick up the pumpkin pie on my way home from work last night. She's not forgiving me for it."

"She will. Don't give up. It'll work out."

"Maybe. So, do you want to stay? I could use a friendly face across the table."

"Wish I could, but I want to get back to my boys."

Justin's phone chirped in his pocket just as he was walking toward the door. He stayed in the foyer and answered.

"Hello?"

"Justin, It's Mac. Is everything okay?"

"We think we might have found something to help clear me. I'm at my lawyer's house, and I'm just getting ready to drive home. How are things there? Did Keri get my note?"

A long sigh blew through the line. "She did. And I'm afraid she's hightailed it right behind you."

"Keri's here? In the city?"

"Yes. I'm worried about her. She said she was

headed to the mission. Will you please go and make sure she's all right?"

Justin's heart nearly exploded from his chest. "I'll get right over there."

"Thank you." The relief in Mac's voice touched a cord in Justin's heart.

"What's up?" Bob's questioning gaze caught his.

He filled him in then dialed the mission. Four rings later, Rick picked up.

"Rick. I need to know if you've seen a short red-head? Her name's Keri."

"Is that you, Justin?" Rick asked.

"Yes," Justin replied shortly. "Keri?"

"She's here. Sitting right across from me, as a matter of fact. Want to talk to her?"

"Thanks." A tide of relief rushed through him and he closed his eyes, willing his heart to slow to normal. It picked up again at the sound of Keri's voice.

"Justin? Where are you?"

"The question is, what are you doing at the mission?"

"Helping out. Waiting for you."

Justin swallowed hard. He could get used to this woman waiting for him. If she was truly his, she'd never have to wait for long. He shook away the images flooding his mind. "All right. I'm coming over there."

"Okay. Oh, Justin wait. I have good news for you."

"What kind of news?"

"A man came into the mission today. Said to tell you that you ministered to him a few months ago and he and his wife are back together and expecting their fourth child."

Pulse pounding in his temples, Justin croaked out, "His name?"

"Huh?"

"The guy's name, Keri! What was it? Is he still there?"

She hesitated. "I'm not sure. Mike, maybe? Just a sec. I put his business card in my jacket. I'll go get it. Hang on."

Justin's heart pounded. *Please, God. Please let it be Ike.*

After what seemed like an eternity, Keri returned to the phone. "Justin, I can't believe this. I put his business card in my jacket, but it's gone. It must have fallen out."

His optimism crashed, but he rallied enough to hope for another option. "Could it have been Ike? Think Keri. This is important."

"You know what, come to think of it. Yes, it was Ike. I remember thinking about Ike, the senator from our state. How'd you know?"

His hands trembled. "Keri…Ike is the only man who can clear my name. I—Is he still there?"

"I'm not sure. I know he said he wanted to go and talk to the men in the residential area. That was about an hour ago."

"Try to find him. I'll be there as soon as I can." He disconnected the call and turned his gaze upon Bob.

"What?" Bob's face screwed up into a questioning expression.

"This may be all over in just a few minutes, my friend. Guess who paid a visit to the mission today?"

"Who?"

"Ike Rawlings. The one man who knows without doubt that I was at the mission all night. Can you drive me to the bus stop? I don't want to drive Mac's truck down there."

"I can drive you."

Justin shook his head. "I'm not taking you away from your family Thanksgiving. I'd rather just get the bus."

"Really, I don't mind."

Justin smiled at his friend. "I do."

Bob grabbed his coat and let his wife know he'd be back. Then he drove Justin to the bus stop. Cold air shot through the car as Justin opened the door and stepped out. "Thanks for everything. Call me just as soon as you have news."

"You can count on it." Bob's lips pressed into a grim line and he fingered the notebook on the seat next to him as Justin shut the car door.

Watching Bob speed away, anxiety bit at Justin and suddenly he remembered Raven's words of the night before. *I think Justin is innocent, but very, very naive.* His ears burned again at the memory of those condescending words. Was he being stupid where his friends were concerned? Was there an outside influence, or was it time to start looking at Bob as a possible suspect? Or Rick? Both had opportunity to influence any of the residents to lie. But what possible reason could either have? It made no sense. He knew these men too well.

By the time he stood alone and shivering at the bus stop, Justin had all but convinced himself there was no way either of his friends would turn on him.

A burst of air filled the silent bus stop as the city bus ground to a halt beside the bench. Exhaust fumes nearly choked Justin. He stepped onto the bus and found a seat. His thoughts pressed forward to the mission and he willed the bus to hurry. If by some chance Ike was still at the mission, Justin knew he'd go with him to the police station to corroborate his story.

His stomach jumped as he looked out the window and watched the street signs as the bus moved deeper into the city. When he transferred to his last bus—the one that would finally drop him a block from the mission, his stomach was twisting with a combination of dread and optimism.

Would it all be over soon?

It was unthinkable that someone could just breeze in and ruin everything in one day. And a holiday at that. After months of covering up, there was no way he could allow it all to unravel. Not now. He was too close. He felt bad for Justin and the boys. He really did. But nothing mattered more than keeping his wife. If he hadn't taken care of Amelia, she would have told. Ruined everything he'd built. And for what? Money? Money for silence. There was only one thing to do…get rid of the evidence. Then he'd worry about finding the tape. He was getting closer. Justin would open up soon and reveal his hiding place… It was only a matter of time.

Chapter Fourteen

Pity clenched Keri's stomach at the sight of Justin's hopeful face as he shot through the mission door. She'd tried. Everyone could attest to that. But she'd failed to find Ike—the one person who could clear Justin. Even though she knew she couldn't have done anything to change the situation, she felt as though she'd let him down.

The light faded from his blue eyes as he studied her face. Disappointment lined his features. "He's gone." The words weren't so much a question as a deflated statement of wretched fact.

She nodded. A groan wrenched from Justin and he dropped into a metal chair, his fingers plunging into his thick hair. Keri knelt on the concrete floor and ran her hand over his hair. Despair thickened the air between them.

"Oh, Justin. I'm so sorry. He was already gone by the time I went looking for him."

He shook his head and pressed his hand to her shoulder. "It's not your fault." A hopeful light brightened his blue eyes. "He didn't say where he's staying, did he?"

Keri shook her head. "If he did, I didn't catch the name of the hotel."

Justin's breath left him in a whoosh. He raised his arms and let them slap back to his thighs. "Well, I guess that's that."

The lines of defeat etched on his face speared her already raw heart.

"I guess we might as well go back to the cabin. There's nothing we can do here." He barely spoke above a whisper.

She nodded and rose.

"Justin!" Rick's voice called out. Keri clenched her fists at her sides. The man irritated her. Plain and simple.

Justin smiled and accepted the quick hug his friend offered. "Rick. I hear Ike was here."

"Sorry we couldn't stop him."

Keri didn't buy it. Not for one minute. "He introduced himself to us earlier, remember? I'm surprised the name didn't ring a bell while he was here," she said, knowing her face betrayed her skepticism, but not caring if it did. Rick should have known. If anyone knew Ike Rawlings was the man who could give Justin an alibi, it was this man.

Rick's expression fell. He rubbed his jaw. "So many of them come and go through this place, I can't keep them straight. Sorry, man."

"Yeah, sure. You couldn't help it."

Keri understood the despair in Justin's voice. His hopes had hinged on finding Ike. What was going to happen now?

Rick clapped Justin on the shoulder. "Come back to

my office and have a cup of coffee with me. Your girl here worked herself to the bone today. I don't know what we'd have done without her."

Justin didn't bother to set him straight. Keri was about to do just that when Justin spoke. "We can't stick around, Rick. I need to get Keri back to her family for Thanksgiving."

Did she imagine it, or did Rick's eyes flash with anger? The next instant he smiled warmly and nodded understanding.

"So let me call a cab for you," Rick offered.

Justin turned to Keri. "Where's your Jeep?"

"I left it at a gas station off the highway." She gave him the exit number. "The man there used to be one of your residents, from what I understand."

Justin's brow rose. "Oh?"

"Mike something or other. That must be why I confused the names. Ike—Mike."

"Mike…" Justin's face registered a mind trying hard to remember.

"This guy got drunk and slammed into a concrete wall, only instead of killing himself, he took out his family."

"Oh…Mike."

The compassion reflected in Justin's eyes shamed Keri, and the shame angered her all the more.

"He served his time for what he did," Justin said softly. "And trust me, he'll never be free from what he's done." His eyes grazed her face with a tenderness that nearly melted her anger. Keri knew he understood why she was angry at the mere mention of this man's actions.

A snort from Rick captured her attention. "Maybe. Some find the Lord here, but for every one we reach, there are five who end up back on the street sucking down a bottle of cheap wine—and only God knows where they find the money."

Keri swallowed with difficulty around a knot in her throat. "Everyone is capable of change," she croaked out.

The admission cost her plenty. If she really believed that anyone was capable of change, then she had no crutch with which to support her crippling bitterness. Because if anyone could change, then so could the man who killed her mother, so could Mike, so could Junior Conner, so could she...

Tears stung her eyes, but she blinked them away and steeled her heart. She couldn't break down now. She wasn't ready to surrender the emotions that had driven her for ten years. Her cause. The force behind her entire life's work as a cop. Getting drunks off the road—that was her passion. Without anger to prod her, she wasn't sure if she'd continue the fight. Didn't know if she even could.

Justin reached out and laced his fingers with hers. He gave her hand a reassuring squeeze and smiled. Then he turned to Rick. "We need to go. Can I use the phone to call a cab?"

Keri frowned. "Where's Dad's truck?"

"I left it at Bob's. We'll need to go over and pick it up."

"How about I drive you over there while Keri goes to get her Jeep?" Rick's voice intruded.

Justin seemed to consider the suggestion. Then he shook his head. "I appreciate the offer. But I want to personally make sure she makes it back to her Jeep safely."

His fingers remained laced with hers, and she couldn't help but feel secure and protected. If only the moment were right for her to lay her head against his chest, close her eyes and breathe in the musky scent of his aftershave. The look in his eyes revealed plainly that he, too, wished they were alone. When he winked at her, a promise of things to come, she felt her skin warm. But rather than averting her gaze in timidity, she smiled. He squeezed her hand again then focused on Rick. "So...your phone?"

Rick motioned toward his office in the back of the room. They walked together and Rick called a cab, then replaced the receiver and motioned for Keri and Justin to sit down in the seats across from his desk.

"That coffee sounds good," Justin said. Keri sensed his tension and wondered if coffee was the best decision.

Rising, Rick moved to the coffeepot in the corner of his office. He turned and raised the pot toward Keri. She shook her head.

"How is Joy?" Justin asked, breaking the silence as Rick set a steaming mug on his desk.

A hefty sigh emanated from deep in Rick's chest. "The same. She has good days and bad days." He shrugged and dropped back into his seat.

"Give her my love, will you?"

"Thanks, I will."

Keri's gaze swept Rick's left hand. No ring. So who was Joy? A sister, friend...dog? Then she blushed as she lifted her eyes to find him staring back at her, amusement crinkling the lines around his mouth.

"Joy is my wife. I don't wear a wedding ring down here because we don't typically flaunt any kind of jewelry. It's not a good idea. Justin was the only one who wore his ring like a shield."

"A shield?" Keri turned to Justin. His brow furrowed.

"The ladies throw themselves at him. Apparently those eyes are irresistible."

"That's enough, Rick." As if on cue, Justin searched Keri's face. Unable to look away, Keri sat transfixed by his gaze. Rick was right about one thing…those eyes were irresistible. "I wore my ring because I was a married man, and I didn't figure anyone was going to try to steal a gold band off my finger."

The door flung open before Rick could reply. A man wearing a suit and an overcoat sprinted into the room.

Justin shot to his feet. "Bob!"

"Call 911," the man said without acknowledging Justin.

"What's wrong?" Justin made a grab for his coat off the back of his chair and shrugged into it as he walked toward the door.

"There's a man in the alley about a block away. He's been stabbed."

"Is he alive?" Rick asked, as he reached for the phone.

"Barely. I'm going back down there to wait for the ambulance. Make sure you direct them to the alley."

Justin followed, so Keri did, too, her heart in her throat.

"What are you doing down here, anyway, Bob?" Justin asked as they jogged down the alley.

"I decided to come down here, too, in case this Ike Rawlings is willing to go down to the police station and give a statement. I thought I'd go along and put some pressure on them to drop the charges. What did you find out from him?"

A few feet ahead, Keri made out a body lying in the alley. She squared her shoulders, bracing herself for the sight of blood.

"Ike was already gone by the time I got here," Justin replied, slowing to a walk.

Lights from the screeching ambulance filled the alleyway, blinding Keri, which was just as well, she supposed. The thought of having to face a possibly dead body left her feeling faint. Briarwood had its problems, but in ten years, she could count on one hand the number of times she'd been faced with a dead body. All but one had died of old age. The fifth had been her mother.

"I'm sorry, Justin," Bob said. "I know it had to be hard, getting so close only to have the man slip away. Is there no way you can find him?"

A garbled sound came from Justin. Keri jerked her head around, concern filling every ounce of her body. He stared in horror at the victim.

"Justin, what's wrong?"

He pointed with a trembling finger. "It's Ike."

Justin paced the ER waiting room of the Truman Medical Center, praying diligently…frantically…for Ike to make it. The paramedics had seemed grim. Ike had lost massive amounts of blood. The ER doctors were working on him, but it didn't look good.

Justin glanced across the room, and his heart nearly melted. Keri sat on an orange vinyl love seat, her legs pulled up to her chest, her head resting on her knees. She looked so young and innocent, it was hard to believe she was aiming at being Chief of Police of Briarwood.

As if summoned by his thoughts, she lifted her gaze and found his. His heart picked up at the sleepy smile curving her lips. He strode across the room and sat next to her. Taking hold of her ankles, he pulled her legs across his lap.

"Better?"

She nodded. "Thanks. I must have dozed. Any word?"

A deep sigh pushed out of Justin's chest. He shook his head. "Not yet."

"Rick and Bob?"

"They both left. Rick said he had to go back to the mission and Bob mentioned the diary. He's hoping Amelia's own words will prove my innocence."

Keri nodded, then asked, "Are you planning to wait until the doctor comes out?"

Justin nodded. "I have to, Keri. I can't leave until I know he's all right. I hate the thought that he was injured and possibly killed because of me, just when he's gotten his life back together and his wife is having another baby."

Keri shot him a glance. "What makes you think that he was stabbed because of you? You think someone was trying to keep him from going to the police?"

"Oh, I don't mean someone deliberately tried to shut him up." Although now that she mentioned it, he could see the possibility. "What I meant to say was that he came to the mission to show me he's a success story and to thank me for helping him.

"Bob said he's going to talk to the police and tell them about Ike. I hope Ike will have the chance to give a statement on my behalf. But if not…" Justin sighed deeply. "I'll have to find a way to prove I'm not guilty. Amelia's diary is a good place to start."

"I'm praying for Ike to come through for you, Justin. But if not, I'll help clear your name. You do not deserve to go to prison for a crime you didn't commit."

Justin had waited all week to see confidence in her eyes when she looked at him. He faced it now as it shone from the emerald depths, and it took his breath away. "Keri," he whispered. He slid his hand behind her neck, threading his fingers through the thick locks of curly red hair. Her soft intake of breath fanned his feelings for her, and he pressed her head closer. He leaned forward just as she closed her eyes.

The door at the end of the hall swung open, and Keri turned away, causing his kiss to fall on her cheek. The sight of the surgeon effectively doused the moment. Keri moved her legs from his lap, standing in her stocking feet. Justin stood next to her. At the doctor's grim expression Justin's hopes plummeted.

"I'm sorry to have to tell you, but Mr. Rawlings didn't make it. His liver was punctured and he lost too much blood. We did our best."

The room spun around Justin. From the distance, he heard Keri thanking the doctor and telling him that they didn't know Ike's wife, but that she was staying in a hotel somewhere in the city. Justin felt himself sinking, spiraling into a pit of defeat. He'd been sure that Ike showing up again was a gift from God. Now it appeared that the rug was being pulled out from underneath him. Justin was going to end up flat on his back in a three-by-five cell for the rest of his life— Unless he could find out who Amelia was having the affair with. Who had fathered her baby, and now, who had murdered Ike?

Chapter Fifteen

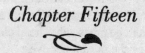

Keri took an alternative route home, opting for the interstate instead of the shorter, back-road path that would allow her to bypass Briarwood on her way to the cabin. She'd decided to stop at the station and grill Abe for any information they'd received about Justin's case.

Before leaving Kansas City, she'd dropped Justin off at Bob's to pick up Mac's truck. She glanced at the digital clock above the radio dials. She'd made good time. The interstate was completely dry, and other than the massive snow banks on the shoulders of the road, no real hint remained that only twenty-four hours before the air had been laden with blinding snow, the road treacherous.

A little after 10:00 p.m., she pulled into Briarwood and headed straight over to the jail. The chief glanced up, and his brow rose when she breezed through the door. "What are you doing here?"

"I could ask you the same thing. I thought Abe would be covering my shifts."

"He got snowed in last night, so we switched. He worked earlier today."

Keri nodded, feeling trapped. If she'd known the chief would be here, she wouldn't have come within a mile of the place. Now there was nothing to do but try to cover her tracks. "So, anything happening lately?"

His gaze narrowed. "Like what?"

"Oh, I don't know. Anything." Inwardly cringing, Keri forced herself to stay calm. She strode to the bulletin board on the wall adjacent the door. Her eyes scanned the board, then came to a sudden stop as she came face-to-face with Justin's picture…blown up to a nine-by-eleven poster.

"What's this?" Keri asked, trying to appear only mildly curious.

"New warrant. Remember him?"

"Of course." Perusing Justin's photo, Keri felt herself drawn to his mouth. The soft lips that had almost kissed hers a few short hours ago. She sighed at the memory of cuddling on his lap while he stroked her hair. The fire in his eyes just before he'd leaned close. She tingled with regret that the almost-kiss had been interrupted.

"Looks about the same as when you two were kids, doesn't he?"

Keri jumped at the chief's voice over her shoulder. She hadn't even noticed him get up and walk over. For crying out loud, what kind of cop was she anyway? A shrug lifted her shoulders as she attempted nonchalance. "I don't know. The eyes might be the same." She forced herself to turn and head over to the desk. She perched on the edge of the metal antique and riffled through papers.

A snort came from the leathery chief.

Knowing she'd better change the subject before she

gave herself away and blew it for Justin, she glanced about, searching for a topic until her gaze rested on the empty cell. "So where's Junior?"

"Finally bonded out."

She expelled an involuntary sniff. "Figures."

"Now, Keri. He's trying to change. Even joined AA."

"Again? Good for him. That should go well for him at trial." At her own sarcastic tone and holier-than-thou attitude, Keri felt a twinge of conscience. Irritation bit at her. She didn't want her feelings to change. Not where Junior Conner was concerned. She gave an impatient sigh and hopped off the desk.

Helping at the mission today had gotten to her. Justin was getting to her. Was God getting through to her? Keri pushed the thought away. Now wasn't the time to ponder the issue.

"So what brings you into town on Thanksgiving?"

The chief's voice came as a welcome interruption from her thoughts. But she scrambled to find a quick answer. She grinned. "Maybe I just missed you."

He snorted. "Don't start flirting with me, little girl."

Embarrassment flooded her cheeks. She sent him her best scowl. "I wasn't…"

He nodded toward the bulletin board. "That Justin Kramer. You two were quite a pair back in the old days, weren't you?"

Defenses on high alert, Keri gave a slight nod. "That was a long time ago."

"You don't suppose he really did it, do you?"

"No way!" She gave herself an inward smack. The answer had come too quick, too confident. As though she had inside info, which of course she did.

Predictably, the chief's bushy brows pushed up, at least an inch above his wire-rimmed glasses. "What makes you so sure?"

Breathe, Keri. Breathe. Don't blow this. She pictured Josh and Billy without a dad and said a miniprayer for wisdom. Justin had promised to turn himself in if the warrant was issued. She had to give him the chance to say goodbye to his boys. There would be no living with herself if she denied him that.

"Well, I'm not one-hundred-percent sure, of course. I just don't think he could do it."

The chief pursed his chubby lips as though deep in thought. "I don't know. It's been a long time since he was that oddball religious kid you had a crush on."

"It was more than a crush. It was love, even back then. And he was not an oddball."

"Maybe so, but scientists tell us a child's personality is developed by the time he or she is six years old. Justin wasn't capable of killing back then, and I have no reason to believe he's capable of such a thing today."

"You could be right, I guess."

Keri shot him a shrouded glance. He wasn't buying it for a second. She could kick herself for not radioing ahead to find out who was working tonight. Abe had all the instincts of a brick. He wouldn't have suspected a thing if she'd shown up during his shift.

But the chief…well he hadn't risen to his position for no reason. Second only to her dad as far as Keri was concerned. His shoes would be hard to fill.

Now there was a topic to get the focus off Justin and her. "So, any more word from the town council about my application?"

"Now, Keri. You can't expect them to work on a holiday."

"No. I suppose not."

Glancing pointedly at her watch, she took a backward step toward the door. "Well, I guess I'll get back to my family. If they didn't leave me a drumstick, you might be called out to stop a family brawl."

The chief let out a chuckle. "Be careful driving. That little highway is still bad—especially with the snow melting and refreezing on the road. You'll have to watch out for black ice."

"Yeah, I know. Thanks."

As she drove slowly back toward the cabin, Keri's thoughts turned to Justin. Had he made it back okay? What would he do now that his only alibi was dead?

Ice pellets sprinkled the ground by the time Keri got back to the cabin. All the way home she'd tried to figure out how to tell Justin about the warrant. So far, she still didn't know how she would do it.

She trudged up the steps and opened the door. A sigh escaped her as the warmth of the snug cabin drew her in. The room was empty, and only the glow of the fireplace provided any light.

A rush of laughter entered the living room through the kitchen door. She smiled, making out the distinct voices of Dad, Denni, Raven and Ruth. She'd join them in a minute, but for now, she needed to distance herself from their questions, to sort through the events of the day.

So many things had happened since she'd left the cabin hours earlier, leaving her overwhelmed and fighting a screaming headache. She leaned her forehead against the mantel and closed her eyes.

"I thought you'd never get home." Justin's low murmur next to her ear oozed over her like warm honey, and she felt the pressure of gentle but firm hands on her shoulders, massaging upward to her neck.

"I didn't see you," Keri said, allowing her muscles to loosen under Justin's expert attention.

"I was checking on the boys."

"How'd they enjoy their Thanksgiving?"

"They loved it. Josh won the wishbone pull."

Keri smiled. "Good. He needed to win."

"I agree. But I'm afraid Billy didn't see it that way."

It struck Keri that they were discussing the boys in the manner of parents sharing at the end of a typical day. An aching sense of longing crept through her middle. She almost groaned out the desperation growing within her. She shook her head. "You can't go away. Not again."

Surrendering to the pressure of his hands on her shoulders as he turned her to face him, Keri braced herself. Now was time for honesty. No more pretending. She had adored and hero-worshipped Justin-the-boy, but she now found herself head over heels in love with Justin-the-man.

Wordlessly, she took in the sight of his chiseled cheekbones, his flawless square jaw accented by the flicker of firelight. He was like a statue. A beautiful work of art.

Outwardly, a masterpiece crafted by a loving creator, inwardly, molded by a potter's hands into a vessel of honor. But Justin went beyond that. He was a man broken by circumstances and yet still willing to serve.

She took a step back. She wasn't good enough for this man. She'd never been good enough for him and never would be. Helplessly she shook her head. "Justin."

Slowly, his hands moved down her arms and slipped around her waist. He pulled her to him. "What's wrong?"

Tears stung her eyes and she tore herself away from the intensity of his gaze. "Nothing. I just…this isn't right."

"Yes, it is." A smile tipped the corners of his lips. "This is destiny. It's always been you and me."

Not always.

She didn't voice the words, but they must have shown in her eyes, for a wave of sorrow washed across Justin's face. He lowered his head, whispering against her lips, "Keri, I'm so sorry. I'd give anything if I could go back."

His strong arms pulled her closer as his mouth covered hers for the sequel to the kiss they'd shared as children. But far from the quick brush of lips that had occurred on that summer day fifteen years earlier, this kiss awoke every sense in Keri's body. She pressed against him as he cradled her.

He lifted his head and gathered a breath. His eyes searched her face, then he reclaimed her lips…lingering. Keri's mind swirled and time and place lost meaning as she stood locked in Justin's embrace—the reality of their moment surpassing every dream she'd ever had.

A low wolf whistle filled the room, a rude awaking to the heady mist swirling about Keri's brain.

Rather than jerking away as though ashamed, Justin slowly lifted his head. He smiled. "It's probably a good thing," he whispered for Keri's ears alone. She flushed hot at the implication, but she had to agree. Despite her lack of romantic experience, she knew temptation lurked very near, and they'd have to be careful now that they knew the wonder of being in each other's arms.

Trying to compose herself, she gathered a long, slow breath and turned to face her family.

"I guess that solves our question." Raven's gaze focused on Denni.

"Yeah," Denni responded. "No doubt about it. Justin definitely kissed her."

"This was the first time," Keri blurted.

Denni grinned at Raven.

"Well, technically, it's not the *first* time," Justin reminded.

Raven chortled. "Oh, really?"

"We were kids then," Keri shot back, wishing for all she was worth that Denni and Raven would just go away and mind their own business.

Denni threw back her head and let up nearly hysterical laughter. "Does a childhood kiss count, Raven?"

Barely able to speak through her mirth, Raven shook her head. "Nope. You were right. As of dinnertime today, they hadn't kissed."

Dad gave a disgusted grunt. "You girls stop teasing your sister."

At that admonishment, all three girls burst into laughter. "Now, I haven't heard that in ages." Denni walked across the room and gathered Keri into a tight hug. "It's good to see you, honey." She spoke in motherly tones.

Keri smiled. That was Denni. The maternal one. No wonder she felt the need to take in displaced eighteen-year-old former foster-care girls.

"How long are you staying?" Keri asked her sister, as her heart filled with a longing to sit alone with her and pour out the feelings and events of the past few days.

"We're leaving in the morning. Shelly has to be at work tomorrow night."

"Shelly?"

"One of my girls. Remember, I asked if I could bring company?

"Oh, yeah. Where is she?"

"Bunking in Ruth's room. She went on to bed about an hour ago. You'll meet her at breakfast."

As if on cue, Ruth yawned broadly. She leaned over and kissed Mac on the cheek.

"Now that our girl is home, I suppose I should hit the sack myself. I'm leaving at the crack of dawn. There's no telling what shape my café is in. I don't know what I was thinking leaving it in Doris's hands. One of these days I need to get myself some reliable help."

"I'll walk you to your room, Ruthie." Mac followed his fiancée.

Justin's arm encircled Keri's shoulders, and her heart jumped as she turned her head to smile up at him.

"I'm going to bed, too," he said. "Your dad's bunking with the boys and me tonight so you three girls get the living room."

Raven cleared her throat loudly and nudged Denni. Denni's lips curved into a wry smile. "We'll just be in the kitchen." Laughing, the two sisters linked arms and ducked out of the room, leaving Keri and Justin alone once more.

"Finally, I have you all to myself again." Justin pulled her close for a long, gentle kiss. Keri sensed that he held himself in check, not allowing his emotions free rein as he had earlier. He pulled away and pressed a kiss to her forehead before dropping his hands.

"Justin, I need to tell you something."

"What is it, honey?" He laced his fingers through her hair.

Keri closed her eyes, gathering a breath for strength. "I went by the station. They've issued a warrant for your arrest."

His face blanched and he released Keri. "Does the chief know I'm here?"

She shook her head. "I wanted to give you a little time with the boys. You said you'd turn yourself in."

He nodded. "Well, then I guess that's that. I'll turn myself in tomorrow."

"Justin…"

Pulling her close, he buried his face in the curve of her neck. She stroked his hair, trying to comfort him. But her heart cried out. *Why?*

From the chair by the fireplace, Justin watched the rise and fall of Keri's shoulders as she dozed on the couch. She had awakened early this morning after only a couple of hours of sleep, and eaten breakfast with her sisters before they each left for their respective homes— Raven in Kansas City. Denni and Shelley in Rolla.

Justin's night had been sleepless as his mind whirled in a million different directions. How was he going to tell them?

He heard the padding of little feet and turned to find Josh, his locks standing on end, fists rubbing the sleep from his eyes.

"Morning, sport," Justin said around a sudden lump

in his throat. He pulled the boy into his lap. This might be the only chance he had left to talk to Josh about what he had read in Amelia's diary. "I'm glad you're up. I need to talk to you about something."

"Did I do something wrong?"

With a stroke of his hand, Justin moved a lock of hair from the boy's forehead. "No, son. You're not in trouble."

"Okay." But he didn't seem convinced.

With a quick prayer for guidance, Justin gave what he hoped was a reassuring smile. "I went to our house yesterday."

Josh frowned. "Why? I like it better here."

"I know. I went because I thought I might be able to find out who killed your mom."

Hope lit the boy's eyes. "Did you?"

"No."

"Oh. Then we still have to hide from the police so they don't catch you."

Alarm shot through Justin. "Is that what you thought we were doing?"

He nodded. "I saw on TV at home. They think you did it."

"Oh, Josh. I'm sorry. I didn't want you to know."

Josh shrugged. "It's okay. I know you didn't do it."

Startled into the opportunity to carry the conversation into the right direction, Justin blurted, "Do you know who did?"

The boy dropped his gaze, shaking his head.

"Do you think you *might* know?"

A shrug lifted Josh's shoulders.

Justin took him by the arms and met him at eye

level. "Josh, did you hide your mom's diary under your toy box?"

Fear flashed in Josh's eyes as he nodded.

"Why?"

"I saw something, and I didn't want you to read Mom's diary and get mad at what she did."

"It's okay. What did you see?"

A shudder moved through Josh's body, and Justin pulled him close, despite a desire to shake the words out of him. "Don't be scared. I won't let anything happen to you. What did you see?"

"Uncle Bob…"

Shock jolted through Justin like a bolt of lightning. "You saw Uncle Bob hurting Mom?"

"No." Josh pulled away, tears running down his face. "I saw him kissing her."

Disbelief sank razor-sharp claws in Justin's gut and his limbs grew weak. Fighting to control his anger and disappointment, he swallowed hard. "Did Bob see you?"

As though overwhelmed with emotion, Josh flung himself back into Justin's arms and buried his face in Justin's shoulder. He shook his head. "I ran away," came the muffled reply.

Justin's heart pounded in his chest and grief nearly overcame him. Bob and Amelia having an affair? And his son had been witness to one of their moments of indiscretion. In their home. His home! He wouldn't have put anything past Amelia…but Bob? Anger shot through him. He'd known for a year that Bob and his own wife were barely on speaking terms, but this had never occurred to him. Had Bob killed Amelia to keep her quiet about the baby?

Rubbing his hand over Josh's head, Justin held the boy close. He wouldn't press him about overhearing Amelia's conversation with Bob, presumably, that she was pregnant. No wonder Bob had been so hesitant about the diary.

The diary! Nausea hit him full in the gut. He'd given it to Bob, of all people. Now there was no proof that Justin might be innocent. Nothing to cast suspicion on anyone else.

Chapter Sixteen

"Justin?"

At the sound of Keri's voice, Justin eased his gaze away from the hypnotic pull of the fire. His heart caught in his throat at the sight of her resting on one elbow, eyes droopy from sleep. This was a picture he definitely wanted to wake up to each morning.

"Hi, sleepyhead." He smiled.

A frown creased her brow. "What's wrong?" She sat up fully, pushing at the afghan covering her.

"What do you mean?"

"You were staring into the fire just now."

Leaning forward, he rested his elbows on his knees and interlocked his fingers. He related the information his son had revealed. Keri's eyes grew wide, her face red with anger. "Do you think Bob ran in and told us to call 911 for Ike to cover up what he'd done?"

Justin shrugged. "I don't know. It seems likely. If he killed Amelia, he wouldn't want to become number two on the list of possible suspects. He'd have to keep the police on my trail."

"That rotten jerk!" Keri shot to her feet and stomped to the fireplace. She grabbed the poker and jabbed at a log. The action caused a round of sparks to fly up from the flaming coals—matching the sparks shooting from Keri. She replaced the poker and turned. "And I've been suspecting Rick this whole time."

"Why would you suspect him?" Justin reached for her hand and pulled her onto the footstool in front of his chair until they faced each other, their knees pressed together.

"I don't know. He just rubs me the wrong way. I know that's not a good reason to suspect someone of murder and a cover-up, but I was looking at possible suspects. He was the only one I could think of."

Justin grinned and kissed her quickly. "Well, I think we can safely rule him out. As a matter of fact, I think I'd better call him and warn him about Bob. Plus, I want to make sure they found Ike's wife."

Keri drew back, worry clouding her eyes. "Are you sure you should trust Rick just yet?"

"I thought you agreed you didn't have a good reason to suspect him." A wry smile tipped the corners of his lips. "Besides, I'm not such a poor judge of character that I'd be oblivious to both of my best friends stabbing me in the back."

"I'm sorry. Of course you're not. I just…" She hedged, then gave him a sudden smile. "Never mind. I'm being overly cautious, I'm sure."

"Don't apologize. I think it's sweet. I haven't had anyone to worry over me since my parents died."

Compassion moved across her face. He pressed his forehead against hers. "We'll get through this and when we do, I hope you'll let me make up for the last fifteen years. I don't ever want to be without you again."

She pulled away, tears shining in her eyes. "Same here."

They moved apart as the kitchen door opened and Mac appeared, followed by Josh and Billy. "We're done with breakfast. Can we watch cartoons?"

"If it's all right with Miss Keri," Justin said, ruffling the tyke's hair.

"I don't see why not," Keri replied with a fond smile at the twins.

Waves of longing swept over Justin at the sight. He prayed that one day soon, they would add Keri to the family. His boys needed her. *He* needed her.

He stood abruptly. "I'm going to go back to my room and make a call." And then he had to have the dreaded conversation with his boys. The one where he told them he was about to be arrested.

"This is Rick."

"Hi. It's me."

"How are you? The police have been crawling all over this place today. Ike died in the hospital."

"I know. I was there."

Rick gave a heavy sigh. "That's all we need…another murder investigation making the people around here nervous."

"Did they find his wife?"

"Yes. She's pretty distraught, as is to be expected. She'll be taking the body back to Chicago for burial as soon as the coroner's office releases it."

"Listen, Rick. I think I might know who killed Amelia."

"Really? Who?"

Justin hesitated, not sure he wanted to reveal this over the phone, but his window of opportunity was quickly shutting. He had no choice. "My son, Josh told me today that he saw Amelia and Bob kissing."

"Bob Landau?" The incredulity in Rick's voice was unmistakable and Justin warmed to the support.

"I know. I found it hard to believe at first, too. But there's more."

"Really?"

"My housekeeper found Amelia's diary in Josh's toy box yesterday. Amelia was apparently pregnant."

Rick hesitated, and Justin heard a quick intake of breath. "She wrote that in her diary?"

"Yeah. And we both know I wasn't the baby's father. But the diary doesn't specifically name the man responsible."

"So do you want me to take the diary to the police?"

"Bob has it."

"Bob? Well, that's not good."

"I took it over to his house yesterday right before I talked to you on the phone." Realization hit him hard. "I suppose he must have driven to the mission and somehow found Ike."

"Yes," Rick breathed as though he was just putting two and two together, as well. "And running into the office like a crazy man was his cover-up for killing the only person who could testify that you didn't leave the mission the night Amelia was killed."

"Exactly," Justin said, defeat thick in his voice.

"I'm really sorry you had to find out one of your best friends betrayed you. Is there anything I can do?"

A heavy sigh leaked through the lines and Justin almost felt sorry for his friend. "Having someone I can trust means the world."

"I love you like a brother. It rips me up thinking about you getting convicted and those kids ending up in foster care. You know, I'd take them in a second if that happens."

Fondness welled up in Justin. "You've no idea how much that means to me, but I've taken care of that. Keri will be raising them with her dad."

"Ahh, I see."

Justin frowned. Did he detect a note of hurt in Rick's tone?

"I'd better go. The boys are about to put in a video, and I want to explain things to them before I turn myself in."

"Did you say they were watching a video?"

"Yes. You know how crazy they are about John Wayne movies. We managed to grab a few of them before we left home. They've been a godsend. Believe me. And more than likely they're the only things from home they'll have for a while."

"Well, they need something to give them some normalcy right now."

Justin disconnected the call and stepped back into the living room. He stopped short at the sight of Keri standing at the door, an older officer on the threshold. Her feet were planted and Justin could see from her belligerent expression that she was spoiling for a fight.

"It's all right, Keri."

The chief eyed him, firmly, leaving no room for rebellion. "I'm taking you in."

A heavy sigh escaped Justin's chest. "I know. I won't fight you."

"Daddy!"

The boys sat huddled together on the couch, wide-eyed. Justin stooped beside the couch. "I'm going to go with the police officer. Not because I did anything wrong, but because they want to ask me some questions."

"When will you be back?" Billy's lips quivered.

"I'm not sure. But I want you to stay here with Miss Keri and do what she and her dad tell you, okay?"

Tears trailed down both boys' cheeks, but they nodded bravely like a couple of troopers. He gathered each in his arms for a long embrace, knowing it might be a while before he would have the opportunity to cuddle the warm bodies close again, smell freshly shampooed curls, kiss sleep-caressed cheeks. He swallowed hard as he tried to control the burning behind his eyes.

Josh's small arms tightened around his neck and he clung until Justin gently held him away. Keri stepped forward and took Josh in her arms. The sight of his son's face buried in Keri's waist clogged Justin's throat.

He stood and faced the officer. "I'm ready."

"I guess Keri's been hiding you at the cabin." Disappointment edged the chief's voice.

"We've been here a couple of days. But as far as we knew there was no arrest warrant until yesterday."

"True enough. But she knew last night."

"I was giving him a chance to say goodbye to his boys, Chief."

"That wasn't your call, Keri-girl."

She grabbed her jacket. "I'm going with you."

"No!" Justin walked across the room and took his own jacket from the coat rack. "I don't want you to go. Stay with the boys. They need you more than I do."

Stepping closer, she wrapped her arms around his neck, apparently heedless of their audience. It was the first time she'd initiated contact and a tide of joy washed over Justin as he held her tight. "Just be careful," she said close to his ear, her breath tickling the nape of his neck. "I don't want to raise them without their father."

"I'll do my best," he whispered. "I love you."

She pulled back and captured his gaze. "I love you, too, Justin Kramer. I always have."

The sweetness of their kiss made Justin's heart sing with hope. But urgency nipped on the heels of optimism—urgency to find Amelia's killer soon. All he could do now was hope that Rick got through to the detectives and that things were falling into place for his release.

The boys sat together on the couch, sullen and still. Keri understood exactly how they felt. It had been a couple of hours since the chief took Justin in. It would have taken at least an hour to get to Briarwood and another hour to process Justin.

"I have an idea," she said, forcing a cheerful tone she was far from feeling. "Let's watch a cartoon."

"I don't feel like it," Josh said.

"Oh, come on. How about this one?" Keri snatched a tape from the top of the TV and held it up.

"We watched it yesterday," Billy said.

"Funniest one I ever saw," Mac chimed in. "Let's watch it again, we could all use a good laugh."

Keri slid the tape into the VCR and sat between the

boys. Each had snuggled close. Before long, Dad's laughter turned to snoring. A fond smile touched Keri's lips at the sight.

The boys, too, were about to give it up, as evidenced by their wide yawns and drooping eyes. "All right, kiddos," she said, rousing them. "How about a nap?"

The boys offered only mild protest as they slogged down the hallway to their room and virtually fell into bed, asleep as their heads hit their respective pillows.

What beautiful children they were. A thrill raced through her as a thought she'd feared to allow admittance, finally won the battle and sprang front and center in her mind. *Justin will be cleared. Then we'll be married and Billy and Justin will soon be my sons.* Tears burned the back of her throat. She placed her hand softly on first one precious head, then the other.

"Bless these children, Lord," she whispered. "Please keep them safe. I know you have a plan that involves only their good."

If Justin ended up in prison, what prices would these children have to pay en route to their expected end?

Voices intruded from the living room as she stepped out of the boys' room and walked back down the hall. *Justin?*

Her quickly beating heart propelled her forward. Once back in the living room, she stopped short and looked around. Dad's snores were the only sounds in the room besides the voices from the video in the TV. She glanced at the box, ready to turn it off when she realized the scene playing itself out on the screen was far from a cartoon.

She moved close to the TV and sat on the floor. Taking the remote, she did a scan/rewind until she came to the end of the cartoons, where someone had begun recording.

Heart in her throat, Keri watched a woman who could only be Amelia. The woman opened the door and a man stepped through it. A gasp escaped Keri's lips.

Rick. I KNEW it!

"It's about time," Amelia snapped. "Give it to me."

Rick pulled a bag from his jacket pocket. Keri peered closer and scowled. The clear bag contained white powder. She was pretty sure it was cocaine.

Amelia reached, but Rick jerked it back. "All in good time," he taunted.

Revulsion twisted Keri's gut as the woman shifted tactics, she slithered close and wrapped her arms about his waist. Clearly moved, Rick kissed her soundly and passionately.

"Now, how about that bag?" Amelia said, her voice husky as she made a grab for the loot still hidden in his hand.

Oh, Justin. How could you have ever married a woman like that?

"First we need to discuss these terms of yours," he said. His other hand wrapped around her wrist, and he pushed her from him.

"There's nothing to discuss. I like the way things have been going." She turned around, and a sly smile slid over her lips, though her back was to Rick.

Keri frowned. The woman was stupid enough to play a dangerous game with a man like Rick, but obviously smart enough to know she could be in danger and should therefore videotape the encounter. Even if it made her look bad—which it did.

"I've decided you're going to have to get off the drugs."

Amelia gave a nervous laugh. "You've decided that? Who are you to tell me what to do, Rick? I think we both know who holds the cards here."

"Don't push me, darling." The chill in his voice sent an icy shiver down Keri's spine.

"Don't threaten me, *darling*."

Rick moved closer. His face was twisted and red. Anger radiated from him like fog over a field on a humid, summer morning. Keri tensed. She didn't want to watch a murder, but she desperately needed to see how this played out, if it indeed held the key to Justin's freedom. Her instincts screamed for her to stay with it. Not that anything could have induced her to turn off this tape in a million years.

"Now you listen here, you little tramp. That's my baby you're carrying and I'm not going to give my Joy a deformed kid. You're going to get clean and stay that way until the baby is born. Is that clear?"

"So you can take all the drugs you want, and I just get to watch? Forget it. Give me that bag." Keri recognized the panic of a junkie in bad need of a fix.

"It's not going to happen."

"I think you're forgetting one very important detail."

"I'm not forgetting anything, sweetheart." Coming from his curled lips, the word sounded like anything but an endearment.

Keri shuddered at the warning in his tone. She longed to caution Amelia to shut up. Not to push him anymore. But of course, she knew better.

"Remember, I saw what I saw. Wouldn't the mission

board be interested to discover how you supplement the pitiful wage you earn as their administrator?"

"Are they going to believe you, doll? Do you really think they'd believe a junkie tramp over a respected member of a thriving church and the minister of mercy to those poor drunks who come in off the street?"

"Do you want to take that chance? Especially now, when your beloved Joy will finally get the baby she's not woman enough to make for herself?"

His hand shot out and grabbed her throat. He pressed her against the wall and moved in so they were nose to nose. "Don't push me, Amelia. Or so help me…"

A strangled *eek* escaped the woman's clenched throat and he let her go. She slithered down the wall and sat hard on the floor.

Rick stared down at her, a sneer marring his face. "Like I said. You're staying clean until the baby is born. And then you're going away with enough money to keep you gone forever. That's the deal, and you're sticking to it."

A guttural shriek rose from Amelia. At the animalistic cry, Keri nearly jumped from her skin.

"What's that?" Dad's startled shout added to Keri's tension.

"Shh. Dad, it's okay." She paused the tape. "Come look at what's on the end of the boys' cartoon tape. It looks like I was right about Rick after all. Somehow, Justin's wife had the gumption and brains to hide a camera and tape this conversation. So far I've discovered that the baby she's carrying belonged to Rick and that they're both heavily into drugs."

"Rick? Justin's friend?"

"So-called," Keri answered, tasting the bitterness on her tongue. She pressed the button and the figures on screen resumed their movement. Amelia slammed into Rick from behind and he lost hold of the bag. Its contents flew across the room and powdered the floor.

A string of vile words spewed from Rick's mouth. "Do you know how much money you just wasted?"

But Amelia wasn't listening. Disgusted, Keri watched her scrambling to save the drugs. Rick stepped over her. "This is the last time. Take what you can salvage and hope it doesn't mix with whatever is on the floor and kill you."

He squatted down in front of her and grabbed her by the arm to gain her attention. With an impatient grunt Amelia looked him in the eye.

Rick's voice held unmistakable warning. "Get your things packed and write Justin a 'Dear John' letter. I'll make sure he's working at the mission tonight, then I'll be back to take you to your new home where you'll stay clean until my baby is born."

Oblivious to the fact that she'd be dead in a few hours, Amelia failed to notice as Rick slipped out and closed the door behind him.

Gathering a long breath, Keri watched for another minute, then couldn't watch the woman anymore. She shut it off and turned to Dad. "What do you make of all that?"

A smile split Dad's face. "I think Justin is going to be a free man very soon."

Chapter Seventeen

"It's for you."

For the third time in the last twenty minutes, Justin refused the phone call.

"Look, this fellow says he's your lawyer. Sounds like you'd best talk to him."

"Tell him he's fired," Justin grunted.

"You tell him. I ain't your secretary."

Swinging his legs over the side of his cot, Justin sat up. "Fine. I'll introduce you to the real person who ought to be in jail."

The chief snorted as he stood up, the keys to Justin's cell dangling in his fingers.

"The real person who should be in jail, eh? That's a new one. An inmate accusing his lawyer of the crime."

"Yeah, well. I just found out tonight that my lawyer was having an affair with my wife. An affair he conveniently failed to mention to the police."

With a dubious lift of his brow, the chief blew out a short laugh. "Your lawyer was having an affair with your wife?"

"Yes. And just in case you were wondering, the husband's always the last to know."

The chief chuckled, but continued his maddening perusal.

"Put the phone on speaker. Who knows? Maybe I can trick him into confessing something and you'll be a witness."

"Might be fun to see what happens. Sure." He pressed Speaker and nodded at Justin.

"Bob?"

"Justin. What's the big idea refusing my calls? Are you nuts?"

Justin fought to hold his anger in check at the sound of his former friend's voice.

Bob hesitated only an instant, then moved ahead without Justin's reply. "Never mind. I have some news."

Justin braced himself. "I already know Ike's dead."

"Yes, and I'm sorry about that. But this is something else. Ike's wife gave a statement on your behalf."

Despite the situation, Justin's heart jumped. "What sort of statement?"

"Apparently, just before Ike left the mission, he called her at their hotel and told her he'd be late because he needed to go by the police station."

"How'd you find this out? I thought the cops didn't have to tell us anything until the court process starts."

"They don't, but I guess Appling grew a heart or something. He called me. Anyway, do you remember a resident named Brian?"

"Of course. He was close to making a decision for Christ when all this started last week."

"Right. Well, he was at the mission yesterday and

told Ike all about the police suspecting you. So Ike was headed over to the police station when someone jumped him and stabbed him. The police are treating it as a homicide connected with Amelia's case."

A full breath burst from Justin's lungs. Relief, wonder, caution all vied for first place in his mind, until he struggled for clarity. "What does that mean for me, exactly?"

"Well the other good thing is that Ike found out who the two men were who were going to testify against you. Apparently he was convincing enough that when the police started looking around the mission again after the hospital reported Ike's death, one of the men came forward and admitted he was lying—the police cut him a deal if he testified. And Justin…" Silence filtered through the line.

"Yeah?" Justin prodded.

"I don't know how to tell you this, but the man said Rick's the one who paid him off to tell the story. I can only imagine Rick killed Amelia to keep her quiet about the baby. The police are going to double-check about the pregnancy, by the way. It's not in the coroner's report."

A sense of betrayal ripped Justin's gut like a hundred rounds of ammo. "Rick…killed Amelia?" Confusion clouded his mind. "You were *both* having an affair with my wife?" How could he have been so stupid?

Silence lingered on the other end of the line. "What do you mean *I* was having an affair with her?"

"Don't even bother to deny it, Bob." A heavy weight of grief over his friend's betrayal pressed on Justin and his shoulders slumped.

"I have to deny it, Justin. It's simply not true. How could you think something like that? I love my wife. We've had some tough times this year trying to get pregnant, but I wouldn't cheat."

"Josh said he saw you and Amelia. Kissing."

"Kissing?" Bob hedged, and Justin braced himself for the forthcoming confession. "I didn't know Josh was there."

"Now you know."

"You have to believe me when I tell you that I had nothing to do with that kiss. She came on to me once last spring. Remember that barbecue we had a couple of weeks after we moved into the house?"

Justin remembered. It was during one of Amelia's nondrug periods. She had actually joined the family at the Landaus'.

"When my wife took you inside to show you the room we're fixing up for the baby we hope to have really soon, Amelia went to work on me. I admit I was flattered and probably didn't discourage her flirting quickly enough, but when she kissed me, I set her straight. I didn't kiss her back. I promise. And I surely didn't know Josh saw it."

The confession rang true and Justin believed him. Perhaps if Amelia had been a real wife and theirs had been a real marriage, the explanation might have been harder to swallow. But Amelia had been adulterous and conniving. It all fit. "All right. One more question."

"What's that?"

"Why were you in the alley last night in the first place?"

"I told you, I wanted to be there just in case Ike was willing to go to the police on your behalf."

"I know. But why the alley? Why were you the one to find him?"

"I've been using your parking space in the garage so I don't have to take a bus down to the mission for pro bono cases. The garage is behind the mission, so obviously I'd have to take the alley to get there. I almost ran over Ike." He paused. "Now that I think about it, putting those two things together, it did make it look like I was guilty."

"I'm sorry, Bob. I didn't know what to believe."

"Let's concentrate on putting this whole thing to rest."

"Have they picked up Rick?"

"No. They're still looking for him."

"Bob, I need to know if they've dropped the charges against me."

"Yes. You're a free man."

Justin wanted to shout. To praise… Mostly he wanted to floor it to the cabin, gather up his sons and let them know it was over. The running, the fear. Next he wanted to get down on one knee and propose marriage to the woman of his heart. But for now he had to take one step at a time.

"Justin? Did you hear me?"

"Yeah, I heard. I'm a little overwhelmed. I want to thank you for all you've done for me. And listen, Bob, I want to make this up to you when I get back. I should have known better."

"I would have felt the same way in your shoes. Trust me." He gave a low chuckle. "It'll be good to wipe the racquetball court with you again, though."

"You're on." Justin grinned and disconnected the line. He glanced up and met the chief's gaze. "Well?"

"We're still waiting for the call from KCPD. When they confirm your friend's story, you'll be free to go. In the meantime, I'm afraid I'll have to lock you back up."

"Chief Manning! Keri and my boys are probably worried sick about me. At least drive me out there so I can let her know I'm okay. Do it for Keri's sake if not for mine."

Chief Manning hesitated, then scowled, but gave a quick nod. "All right. But only because I don't want her to worry. She has enough to think about now that she's out of a job."

They headed out the door toward the squad car. "What do you mean by that?" Justin asked.

"Aiding and abetting."

Justin got into the passenger side and shut the door. "Keri's the best thing that's ever happened to this town. Firing her would be a big mistake."

"She should have told me you were at the cabin when she found out about the warrant."

"That's a little harsh, don't you think? She was only giving me a little time to explain things to the boys." Justin's heart plummeted at the thought that he'd cost Keri not only the chance to advance into the position she'd dreamed of, but even the job she had.

The older man regarded Justin sternly. "What about you? Is there room in your life for her?"

"I plan to ask her to marry me."

"Well, then. I guess you have me to thank." He grinned. "Now she doesn't have to choose between her career and the man she loves."

"You won't arrest her for aiding and abetting?"

He received a deep scowl. "No point in that."

Justin breathed a sigh of relief, grateful that it was all going to be over very soon.

Keri set the phone back on the charger, frustration growling in her throat. Dad should have asked how to work the cell phone before he let the battery die out completely.

Grabbing the keys to Mac's truck from the key holder next to the door, she turned. "I'm taking this tape to the chief."

"Why don't you stay here with the boys and let me do that?" Dad replied.

A smile curved Keri's lips. "I want to see Justin." She snatched her jacket from the peg by the door and shrugged it on. "Keep your phone charging, and I'll try to call you in a few hours."

Dad walked her to the door. He gathered her into a tight embrace. "My girl. I know how hard these years have been since your mother died. I'm glad you stuck around here when your sisters stayed away. Not that I blame them."

Giving him a squeeze, Keri pulled back and smiled. "I wanted to stay, Dad. My life is in Briarwood."

"Is it?"

A wistful sigh escaped her, and she averted her gaze.

Leaning forward, Dad pressed a kiss to her forehead. "It *was* here. Now I think it's wherever Justin and the boys are. But don't you worry about me. I have my Ruthie. I want you to live your life with the man God intended for you. The fact that I'm going to be an instant grandpa is an added bonus."

Keri grinned. "All right, Gramps, I better get this

tape into town so we can work on clearing my future husband, who—by the way—has yet to propose."

"He will." He sent her a wink and opened the door.

She stepped onto the porch and shivered. "Close the door, Dad. It's freezing out here. You don't want to heat the outdoors."

Dad chuckled. "Be careful."

The door closed and Keri carefully maneuvered the icy steps. She walked the few yards to the truck then stopped short, gasping in surprise.

"Hi, Keri."

Rick stood, a charming smile carefully pasted across his face. A duffel bag was slung jauntily over his shoulder. The sight of it caused a nervous chill to slide down Keri's spine. Rick blew out a puff of smoke, and Keri noticed the glow of a lit cigarette between his fingers. "I have some news for Justin." He tossed his cigarette to the ground, not bothering to crush it with his boot.

"H-he's not here." Keri slowly hid the tape behind her back. How had he driven up without her seeing his lights? As a matter of fact, she looked around and didn't see a car. He must have parked out of the way and walked up.

"Oh, that's right. The poor man has turned himself in for a crime he didn't commit."

"Wh-what do you mean?" Her question didn't sound authentic even to her own ears.

Rick's brow rose and Keri cringed. She'd definitely lost her edge. It was just as well she'd decided to give up police work.

His glance slid down her and then rested on her arm. "Where were you headed in the middle of the night?"

"I—uh—I was going to visit Justin, actually."

"I see." He took another look at her arm. "So what's that behind your back?"

"Huh?" Keri cringed. Frantically, she searched her brain, trying to come up with a plan. There was no way she could tuck the tape under her jacket without him seeing. She had no recourse but to show him and try to bluff her way out of it. Slowly, she brought her arm around.

"A tape?" Cold suspicion sharpened his tone.

Keri forced a short laugh. "Those boys of Justin's. They watch that tape over and over. I'm going to conveniently forget I left it in the truck. It's driving me nuts. I mean a cartoon rabbit can only take a right turn at Albuquerque so many times before it stops being funny. Right? "

He laughed with her, but Keri recognized it for what it was. He wasn't buying it for a second. "Yeah, the thing is, I'm partial to that episode. How about we go inside and watch it together? Maybe it'll be a bonding experience. Justin's best friend and his best girl getting to know each other. Doesn't that sound cozy?"

"How about we take a rain check on that? Are you hungry after that long drive? We're still up to our necks in food from yesterday's meal."

"Sure. Let's go inside and I'll have a bite to eat, then."

Keri turned, praying for wisdom. She could hear his breathing…heavy and quick. "You know, you really should give up smoking, Rick. Your breathing sounds pretty bad."

"Thanks, I'll keep that in mind."

She opened the door, but stopped short as Rick loomed over her from behind—so close she could feel his warm breath against her neck. His voice was low, and a definite threat chilled his tone. "You're not fooling me, you know. Give me the tape."

With a resigned sigh, she turned around, still standing in the doorway. He was holding a gun. "How did you know where to find us?"

He snatched the tape from her hand. "Justin told me you and he were childhood sweethearts and that the boys were with you. I put two and two together and looked up his aunt in Kansas City from Justin's computer address book at the mission."

Alarm seized Keri. "Did you hurt her?"

"I didn't have to. The old hag was more than willing to give me any information she could about him. She thought I was a detective. Drew me a map to the cabin."

"So much for family loyalty."

"So let's go inside. I'm getting cold, and cold makes me cranky."

Keri snorted. "Well, we wouldn't want that, would we?"

"No. Trust me, you wouldn't."

"How do you plan to come out of this without implicating yourself, Rick?" Keep him talking.

"There's going to be an unfortunate fire. You know, you have to clean chimneys or burning wood can cause a flue fire. You were very careless, Keri."

"Wouldn't it be easier just to shoot me?"

"They might find the casing."

"So why should I be afraid of that gun?"

"I could always change my mind."

The kitchen door opened. "Keri, what are you doing?"

Keri felt pressure against her back. "Dad, meet Rick."

"The pleasure's all mine." Rick said sardonically.

"What's going on here?"

"Rick came for his tape."

"Well, he's not getting it!"

Rick held tightly to Keri and waved the gun toward Mac. "Actually, I already have it."

"Take it then, and get out of here."

A spurt of laughter left his lips. "If only it were that easy." He slid the duffel bag from his shoulder and tossed it onto the floor at Keri's feet. "Open it," he ordered.

Slowly, she knelt. "Why, Rick? What happened to the man Justin admired so much? The man who worked tirelessly to serve the poor and needy?"

"That man was an idealistic idiot. Just like Justin. The 'poor and needy' will take everything you offer and then destroy you. The only difference is that Justin didn't have to learn that the hard way like I did."

Keri unzipped the duffel bag. "What am I looking for here?"

"Get the rope and tie the old man's hands and feet. Start with his feet." He looked at Mac. "Lie down in front of the fireplace."

Keri's gaze darted to her dad. He lay where he'd been instructed and nodded to Keri. "It's okay, Keri-girl. Do it."

Gathering a deep breath, Keri stood and headed

across the room. "Rick, Justin told me about the man who hurt your wife, and I'm truly sorry. But how does what you're doing help that?"

"It doesn't. What I'm doing keeps me out of jail. As far as the people who come to the mission, no one can truly help *them*."

"But why kill Amelia? Especially when she was carrying your baby?"

"I see you watched the tape," he said wryly.

"Yes. Enough to know you supplied Amelia with drugs and that she was pregnant with your baby."

"First of all, don't try to get cute by keeping the ropes loose. I plan to check them. As to Amelia, she wasn't pregnant. She faked the whole thing—even had records made up to look like a doctor's report." He chuckled. "I didn't know she had it in her."

Keri fastened the last rope around her dad's wrists, tight enough to satisfy Rick, but loose enough that they didn't bite into the skin and cause pain. She stayed next to him in an attempt to make Rick believe she was still working on the ropes. She needed to buy some time. Once he tied her up, there was nothing she could do to save any of them.

"Listen, Rick. I understand how it feels to lose someone you love."

He gave her a sardonic smirk, clearly not buying the I-feel-your-pain routine. "I'm sure you do."

"I honestly do. My mother was killed by a drunk driver, and I hated him and all drunks for years."

"Hurry up with those ropes," he growled.

Keri forged ahead, desperately hoping at least something she said would touch a nerve. This is what bitterness did to people—took caring, loving men and turned them into liars, addicts and murderers. Suddenly Keri saw her own heart. What had her bitterness turned her into? Was she really any better than Rick? Tears burned as she silently repented.

"You see, Rick. In my heart I've murdered that man over and over for what he did to my mother." Her voice caught, and Rick's expression changed—for a flash of a second, but Keri could see that her words had had an effect. Even if it was that quick, it was a start. A seed. She pressed forward. "As far as God is concerned, the unforgiveness in my heart is no better than what you've done. We're all sinners. The man who killed my mother, the man who violated your home and your wife." She paused. "You and I. None of us is good. Only Jesus can change a heart."

"Shut up," he said. "I know you're done with that rope by now." He strode across to her and yanked her painfully away from her dad.

He flung her to the ground a few feet away and grabbed the other rope. "Now it's your turn. Don't try anything cute, or I'll put a bullet in your dad's head."

Keri winced as he grabbed her arms none too gently, and jerked them behind her back. Struggling to continue her speech, she gathered her courage and spoke up. "I know you must still love God somewhere in your heart, Rick. Otherwise you wouldn't have stayed at the mission this long. A man with your credentials could have gotten a job anywhere."

A low laugh rumbled from his chest. "Let me tell you why I stayed at the mission. Because my sweet wife turned into an addict—prescription medication—trying to cope with her rape. When the doctors stopped prescribing them, she almost went crazy from withdrawal. I found plenty of people willing to sell me drugs on the street. Then it occurred to me that I was in a position to make a lot of money. I had the perfect cover. And I could keep buying the drugs for Joy without going bankrupt."

"Amelia saw you selling drugs?" Keri sucked in a sharp breath as the ropes bit mercilessly into the soft flesh of her ankles.

"First she heard about me on the street. And then she started nosing around. She caught me making a deal one night. I supplied her with free drugs to shut her up. Pretty soon the affair started and she told me she was pregnant. I knew a baby would be just what it took to perk Joy right up. Maybe even give her a reason to go into rehab. So I convinced Amelia to have the baby and give it up. I planned to tell Joy I had adopted the baby. In her state, she wouldn't have questioned anything."

"But Amelia wasn't being cooperative," Keri prodded as he moved to tie her wrists.

"She got greedy. Started demanding money instead of just the drugs. Money for silence, she called it."

"But why did she pretend to be pregnant?"

"Just one more thing to hold over my head, I suppose. She knew I was getting tired of her demands—and other things."

Keri winced as the ropes pinched her wrists. He stood over her. "Any more questions?"

"What about the boys, Rick? Surely you aren't going to kill innocent children."

Regret crossed his features. "I wish I didn't have to. Truthfully, I was going to be a good friend and offer to take them when Justin went to prison. But I'm afraid there's nothing I can do about that now."

"There is something you can do about it, Rick. There's always a choice."

"Unfortunately, there isn't in this case. My so-called accomplice couldn't stand the pressure and blabbed to the police about me paying him off to lie about Justin leaving the mission that night. That's the last time I trust a drunk."

To hear him speak so callously about framing Justin caused a shudder of revulsion between Keri's shoulder blades, but she knew if she gave in to the outrage, she had no chance of escape. "Remember your former walk with God. Turn back to Him. If God can change my heart, He can change yours."

"Save it, Keri. It's gone too far. There's no hope anymore."

"There's always hope."

"Not for me, sweetheart," he said, gathering up the remaining rope. "The cops are after me. And I don't plan to be taken alive."

Nausea swirled in Keri's stomach. Rick was a man with nothing to lose.

A flicker of lights coming through the front window squelched anything she might have replied. Rick jerked his head up.

Keri breathed a sigh of a prayer. "Like I said, Rick. There's always hope."

"Don't count on it." He sneered down at her and grabbed a rag and a bottle from his bag. Quickly, he

Chapter Eighteen

Justin saw the blaze through the window and his heart tore in his chest. The boys! Keri and Mac! He raced up the steps ahead of the chief. Good thing the old man got out of his way because he'd have run over him if he'd had to.

He slammed through the door, shoved through the rising smoke, and located Keri and Mac on the floor. The chief bolted through the door right behind him, tore off his coat and beat at the flames.

Covering his mouth, Justin headed toward Keri. "Are you okay?" He quickly worked the knots around her wrists.

"I'm okay. Untie Dad," she said as he moved toward her ankles. "I can get that."

Mac's ropes came apart easily. "It's good you came when you did," Mac said, then a fit of coughing seized him. He lumbered to his feet and grabbed a throw rug from the floor. Following the chief's example, he beat at the flames that were slowly losing their malevolent war.

A scream split the cabin, coming from the boys' room. "Josh!" Justin sprinted down the hall and flung himself into the room. Josh sat straight up on the bed, pointing at the window. "He was there! Just like in my dreams. Only this time it was real."

Justin followed his pointing finger. Wind blew in from the open window. His gut clenched.

"Fire's out!" he heard Mac call from the living room.

Keri appeared. "Is Josh okay?"

"He said he saw someone at the window—like his dream. This time he's right. It's open."

"Rick!"

"Rick?"

Without an explanation, Keri tore out of the room.

"Mac, can you stay with the boys?" Justin asked as he sped through the room.

"I have them. Go!"

Justin ran after Keri. He banged through the door in time to see Keri and Rick struggling on the ground.

He headed in their direction. Gunfire blasted the air.

A strangled scream tore at Justin's throat. "Keri!" He reached them just as Keri sat up, gasping for breath.

"Are you okay?"

"I'm fine," she said.

Justin bent and grabbed the gun from the snow-covered ground and handed it to Keri.

Keri drew in a shaky breath and looked up at him. "He pulled out his gun as I tackled him. "Rick?" She felt for a pulse, then expelled a relieved sigh. "He's alive."

Reaching for her, Justin gripped her hand and lifted

her. He gave her a quick hug. "Are you sure you're okay?"

She nodded. "Let's see about him."

Justin knelt beside Rick, fury searing his mind. A sense of betrayal cut like a knife, slicing at his heart. How could this man, his friend, have become an animal without Justin noticing?

Rick moaned and stirred. "Justin."

Straddling the wounded man, Justin grabbed Rick's shirt with enough force to lift his shoulders from the icy ground. "You almost killed my children!"

"Justin, don't lower yourself to his level. Hurting him further won't help anything." Only Keri's voice and her gentle hand on his shoulder prevented Justin from pounding Rick back to unconsciousness.

"Where are you hit?" he growled.

"My leg," came Rick's agonized response.

"Be glad it wasn't through your heart," Keri said. "If you have one."

"I used to have one, but it was ripped out by someone I once tried to help." Rick grimaced, but turned his gaze on Justin. "I hope the same thing doesn't happen to you."

"It won't," Keri spoke up before Justin had a chance to respond.

"I better put something around that wound before you bleed to death." Justin grabbed a handkerchief from his back pocket and tied it tightly around Rick's thigh. "All right. Let's go. I'm not carrying you, so you'll have to lean on me and do the best you can."

Chief Manning met them at the back door. "Take him around to the squad car."

"He's been shot," Keri said.

"I can see that." No trace of sympathy leaked from the chief's tone. "I'll radio ahead to the hospital on the way. I imagine you'll need to come in and give us a statement, Keri. But that can wait until tomorrow."

"Thanks." She put her hand on Rick's arm. "What were you doing by the boys' window? You could have been long gone if Josh hadn't screamed."

A sneer marred Rick's features. "I didn't figure I got the job done in there with Justin showing up when he did. There wasn't time for a real fire." He gave a short laugh. "I was going to light a couple more rags and throw them through the window."

"What stopped you?" Justin asked, knowing full well that God had been the hand to hold back the fire from where his sons were sleeping.

"Call it a momentary touch of conscience." Rick grimaced and faltered a step. "Josh must have seen my flashlight."

"At least you had enough decency left inside of you to stop," Keri said.

"Which proves my point. Doing the decent thing causes nothing but trouble."

Justin helped Rick to the squad car. Once the man was lying on the seat, agony written on every feature, Justin leaned in. "I don't understand any of this, Rick."

"You never have understood, Justin. For you, it really is about wanting to fulfill some higher calling. For me, it never was. It was just a job."

"I don't believe that. At one time you had a passion for the lost. Just as strongly as I have."

"No one has a passion as strong as you. Except

maybe your Girl Friday over there." He snorted. "You're a perfect pair. The mission board will think they're getting a great deal when they offer you my job."

Obviously, there would be no last-hour repentance, no remorse. Justin shook his head. "You're right. We are perfect together. And I hope the board does offer me your job."

He started to close the door on the man who had been responsible for the upheaval in his life for the past four months, the man who had almost killed his beautiful children and the woman he loved.

"Justin?"

Justin moved close again. "Yeah?"

"See that Joy gets some help, will you? I don't know what she'll do without me. She doesn't have anyone to take care of her. None of this is her fault."

Against all reason, Justin was moved with compassion. He nodded. "I'll do what I can."

When he stood, Keri was waiting. He gathered her close. "Thank God, He kept you safe," he said breathing in the familiar peachy scent combined with wood smoke. Keri clung to him.

The chief cleared his throat. "Make sure you come give that statement."

Keri pulled back from Justin's arms. "What now?" she asked the chief. "Is Justin cleared?"

"Charges have been dropped."

Keri looked at Justin, frowning. "You talked to Bob?"

"Let's just say Josh didn't exactly see what he thought he saw."

She grinned. "That clears that right up."

The chief cleared his throat again. "Keri."

"Yeah, Chief?"

"I don't plan to report anything about you giving this young man an extra few hours with his children. He's innocent, and, considering the circumstances, I don't think there's going to be anything to keep you from getting my job."

Keri gave a short laugh, then she shook her head. "I appreciate it, Chief. But I'm going to have to hand in my resignation."

"I thought you might. But are you absolutely sure?" the chief asked. "You'd be doing Briarwood a big favor it you stuck around."

"Absolutely." She turned and smiled at Justin. "I think I'm about to get a better offer. I'll turn in my gear tomorrow when I give my statement."

"All right, then." Chief Manning nodded toward them. "I guess I better get this fella to a doctor."

The squad car slid as it pulled out of the driveway amid a burst of exhaust fumes. It moved slowly down the icy gravel road.

Justin turned to Keri. "I don't get it. You wanted that job more than anything."

"You're wrong." She smiled and stepped closer to him. "What I want more than anything is right in front of me." The look in her eyes sent waves of emotion over him.

"Are you sure?" he whispered.

"More sure than of anything in my entire life. That is, unless I'm reading you all wrong and you're not interested in keeping me around."

"Hmm. Try to escape." Justin grinned.

Wrapping her arms about his neck, Keri snuggled close. "You were right about me using the law to bring significance into my life. I was trying to avenge my mother's death by waging war on all drunk drivers, but I'm ready to stop doing that." She pulled back and captured his gaze once more. "I—I'd really like to work at the mission—with you."

Justin's heart stirred, but his voice refused to work. He looked down into her liquid eyes and lost all rational thought. He did the only thing that came to mind, and covered her lips with his. Their kiss warmed him, erasing the ugliness of the last few months. Years.

Keri pulled back, and Justin finally found his voice.

"Marry me?" he asked.

"You can count on it." Her lips curved in a flirtatious grin. "I'm never letting you out of my sight again."

He chuckled deeply and bent to kiss her once more. They heard the door bang and both glanced toward the cabin.

"Hey, Dad. Why are you kissing Miss Keri?" Billy shouted from the porch.

"Because I'm going to marry her," Justin called back. "What do you think of that?"

Billy let up a whoop. "I told you, Josh!"

Josh remained silent and padded down the steps in only his socks.

"Josh," Justin lightly admonished, sweeping the boy into his arms. "You'll get sick."

"I want to ask Miss Keri something."

"What is it, sweetheart?" Removing her jacket, she laid it over his shivering body.

"If you marry Dad, are you going to be our mom?"

"I'd like to be, if you'll have me."

"The real kind of mom?"

"What do you mean?"

"The kind that makes spaghetti and cookies. And stays home at night and plays games and buys us clothes?"

Keri reached forward and smoothed his curls. "I love you, baby. There's nothing I'd rather do than be your mom and Billy's. And just so you know, I can make a really great pot of spaghetti. And you should taste my chocolate-chip-pumpkin cookies—oh, I know they sound awful, but wait until you bite into one." Her lip trembled slightly as she smiled at Josh. "As for buying your clothes, we'll make that a family affair and let your dad give us his input. How's that sound?"

"Perfect." Josh grinned.

Justin held his son close and smiled at Keri.

"Perfect," he agreed.

"Perfect," she whispered. She looped her arm through his and together they walked back to the cabin.

* * * * *

Dear Reader,

Is God really a God of second chances? Would Jesus have told His disciples to forgive seventy times seven if He Himself were not willing to do the same?

These were the questions probing my mind and heart as I worked on *Reasonable Doubt.* Looking back at the poor choices I've made over the years, and particularly in my late teens and early twenties, I am awed and humbled at the grace God has poured into my life to give me a future and a hope that I don't deserve. His mercies are new and fresh daily. Oh, how grateful I am for that.

The world is so hopeless, so unforgiving, but we have a message to give that there is hope. As Justin and Keri discovered, although poor choices drove them apart, God saw the end from the beginning and brought them back together in order to use them for His glorious purpose.

My prayer as I write this, my first letter to Steeple Hill readers, is that God spoke to your heart through this book, that He assured you that you have His plan and His purpose for you—a future and a hope, new mercies every day.

Until next time, may God bless you and keep you in His care.

Tracey V. Bateman

And now, turn the page for a sneak preview of
SUSPICION OF GUILT,
the second book in
THE MAHONEY SISTERS *miniseries*
by Tracey V. Bateman,
part of Steeple Hill's exciting new line,
Love Inspired Suspense!
On sale in September 2005
from Steeple Hill Books.

Prologue

The night swirled around her. Black, stabbing darkness conjuring terrible shadows from childhood nightmares. Leaves hovered like vampires' capes, suffocating. Fear gripped her. Branches tossed in the breeze—razor-sharp fingers ready to slice her to shreds.

Hurry, hurry, hurry.

A low, half growl, half whine came from the Doberman behind the fence next door. She jerked her head at the sound, heart pounding in her ears like the thrum of a thousand drums.

Shh. "It's okay," she whispered. "Don't give me away. I'm so close to accomplishing my goal." The dog obeyed—watching but silent.

Relief flooded her as she turned back to her task. Denni Mahoney, with all of her sweetness and nice…

Shards of rage pierced her heart at the thought of Denni getting what she wanted. She didn't deserve it.

A mastermind of deception. Denni had fooled them all.

With a shaky hand she reached for the outside faucet. Hesitated. One twist and the broken pipe would send water rushing inside the house instead of flowing to the ground. The basement would flood.

She grasped the faucet tight and gave it a quick turn.

Water spewed.

The Doberman barked.

Her heart rate escalated. She pushed to her feet, gulping down the fear. She crept across the yard. Relief slowly shoved away the terror of night as she found safety.

Chapter One

Shock, disbelief, horror…all vied for first place in Denni Mahoney's chest as she stared at the foot of water standing in her basement. Water. Just…standing there where water was never meant to be. Despair clutched her heart and squeezed the breath from her lungs. She shook her head, pressing her palm to her forehead.

What next?

"We'll get to the bottom of this." Behind her, Detective Reece Corrigan's tone was hard-edged, resolute, but the warmth of his hand on her shoulder evoked a strange sense of comfort.

"You have to admit it definitely could be one of them. Why do you insist that all five of the girls are innocent?"

The warm, comforting fuzzies turned to cold stone. She didn't have to admit any such thing and she was sick of his suspicions being centered on the girls. Anger shoved down the tears clogging her throat, and she shook off his hand.

Standing on the fourth step from the bottom of the basement stairs, Denni watched a hardback book float across the water covering the concrete floor. *A Tale of Two Cities*. A birthday gift from her mom when she'd turned fifteen. Little by little her memories of Mom were being destroyed. It had been ten years since her death, and only photos provided a clear picture of her face anymore.

Denni grimaced and abruptly turned away, but Reece's body on the step above her blocked her flight up. Even when she sent him her fiercest frown, he didn't budge.

She drew in the subtle scent of his spicy aftershave. Understated appeal. She liked that about him. The guy had to know how he affected women—a muscular physique and a masculinity that intimidated Denni, yet left her wishing he'd stay close.

"Well?" he asked, the tension in his voice replaced by a subtle, low tone that seeped over her like a gentle rain.

She gaped, fighting the warmth creeping to her cheeks. "Well what?" she whispered.

"I'm going to have to question them again. Who should I speak with first this time?"

"Oh, Reece," she said, hearing the fatigue in her tone. She was so tired. So very, very tired. "Leave the girls alone, will you? How can you blame them for a flood?"

Her girls. Troubled, ex-foster-care kids who were too old to stay in the system but too young to be out on their own. As a social worker, she had grown tired of seeing so many of these girls end up in public assistance, their own children placed in foster care, so she'd opened a home.

Only five young women lived with her, but if her experiment panned out, she had commitments from several local churches to help buy two more homes, each housing ten girls. Monday she was supposed to host a luncheon for the liaisons from each of these churches. How could she explain to potential sponsors that the cops suspected her girls of sabotage?

Denni glanced back at the basement, searching for escape from the confrontation that was surely to come. It was either hike down the steps and swim through the murky water or face Reese's rock-solid stubbornness. She sighed, knowing there was only one logical choice. She'd have to face him.

Forcing herself away from the sight of so many of her treasures soaked and more than likely ruined, she braced for the coming conflict, a tiresome, constant echo of accusation.

"Admit it," he demanded.

Deliberately, she lifted her gaze and met his, his steely green eyes silently commanding her to accept the possibility.

"I admit only one thing. It looks as though someone is trying to sabotage my efforts to make a nice home for these girls." A sigh pushed from her lungs. "What I can't figure out is why."

Detective Corrigan scowled. "That's what I'm here for, and I have to tell you…"

Denni raised her hand to stop his opinion from flying out of his mouth. "What possible motive could any of them have to sabotage their own home? Where would they go?"

Leaving him to mull over that bit of reasoning, she

scraped against his bomber jacket as she maneuvered around him and marched to the top of the stairs. He followed her into the kitchen.

"That's the one thing I can't put my finger on. It doesn't make a lot of sense, but maybe the person we're dealing with here doesn't think along rational lines."

"All my girls are rational," Denni snapped.

His amusement was more than apparent in the upward curve of his lips. "Then I guess they must take after you," he drawled.

Love Inspired SUSPENSE

RIVETING INSPIRATIONAL ROMANCE

Suspicion of Guilt

by Tracey V. Bateman

The Mahoney Sisters

Someone wants Denni Mahoney's home for troubled young women shut down, but could the threat be coming from inside?

"One of the most talented new storytellers
in Christian fiction."
–CBA bestselling author Karen Kingsbury

Available at your favorite retail outlet.
Only from Steeple Hill Books!

Steeple Hill®

www.SteepleHill.com   LISSOGTVB

Love Inspired
SUSPENSE
RIVETING INSPIRATIONAL ROMANCE

Die Before Nightfall
BY SHIRLEE McCOY

A thirty-five-year-old mystery of tragic love becomes a
very modern-day threat for nurse Raven Stevenson and
her elderly charge's nephew Shane Montgomery.

"A haunting tale of intrigue and twisted motives."
–Christy Award winner Hannah Alexander

Available at your favorite retail outlet.
Only from Steeple Hill Books!

www.SteepleHill.com LISDBNSM

Take 2 inspirational love stories FREE!

PLUS get a FREE surprise gift!

Mail to Steeple Hill Reader Service™

In U.S.	In Canada
3010 Walden Ave.	P.O. Box 609
P.O. Box 1867	Fort Erie, Ontario
Buffalo, NY 14240-1867	L2A 5X3

YES! Please send me 2 free Love Inspired® novels and my free surprise gift. After receiving them, if I don't wish to receive anymore, I can return the shipping statement marked cancel. If I don't cancel, I will receive 4 brand-new novels every month, before they're available in stores! Bill me at the low price of $4.24 each in the U.S. and $4.74 each in Canada, plus 25¢ shipping and handling and applicable sales tax, if any*. That's the complete price and a savings of over 10% off the cover prices—quite a bargain! I understand that accepting the books and gift places me under no obligation ever to buy any books. I can always return a shipment and cancel at any time. Even if I never buy another book from Steeple Hill, the 2 free books and the surprise gift are mine to keep forever.

113 IDN DZ9M
313 IDN DZ9N

Name	(PLEASE PRINT)	
Address	Apt. No.	
City	State/Prov.	Zip/Postal Code

Not valid to current Love Inspired® subscribers.

Want to try two free books from another series?
Call 1-800-873-8635 or visit www.morefreebooks.com.

* Terms and prices are subject to change without notice. Sales tax applicable in New York. Canadian residents will be charged applicable provincial taxes and GST. All orders subject to approval. Offer limited to one per household.

® are registered trademarks owned and used by the trademark owner and its licensee.

INTLI04R   ©2004 Steeple Hill

Love Inspired®

Tiny Blessings

THE TINY BLESSINGS SERIES CONTINUES WITH

ON THE DOORSTEP

BY

DANA CORBIT

A baby on the doorstep of the adoption agency certainly wasn't what Pilar Estes expected to find on her way to work! The search for the boy's mother soon found Pilar working closely with dedicated detective Zach Fletcher. Yet even as they got closer to finding the missing mother, Pilar longed to make Zach and little Gabriel part of her dream family....

Tiny Blessings: Giving thanks for the neediest of God's children, and the families who take them in!

Don't miss ON THE DOORSTEP
On sale September 2005

Available at your favorite retail outlet.

www.SteepleHill.com   LIOTD

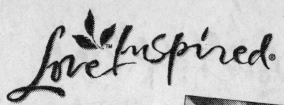

THE TROUBLE
WITH
LACY BROWN

BY

DEBRA CLOPTON

Wives were wanted in tiny Mule Hollow, Texas,
and dedicated-to-staying-single stylist Lacy Brown
was determined to make them beautiful. But her
bachelorette status was threatened when cattleman
Clint Matlock entered her life. Could it be that Lacy
might find herself as Mule Hollow's first new bride?

Don't miss
THE TROUBLE WITH LACY BROWN
On sale September 2005

Available at your favorite retail outlet.

www.SteepleHill.com

LITWLB

THE McKASLIN CLAN

**ENJOY ANOTHER
McKASLIN CLAN STORY
WITH...**

HEAVEN'S
TOUCH

BY

JILLIAN HART

After a combat accident, Special Forces soldier
Ben McKaslin returned home to recuperate, and ran
into his old friend Cadence Chapman. With his
career in tatters and his life on hold, he couldn't
allow himself to fall for her. But Cadence—and
God—had other plans for Ben....

**The McKaslin Clan: Ensconced in a quaint mountain town
overlooking the vast Montana plains, the McKaslins rejoice
in the powerful bonds of faith, family...and forever love.**

Don't miss HEAVEN'S TOUCH
On sale September 2005

Available at your favorite retail outlet.

www.SteepleHill.com   LIHTJH